CHARADE BOOK TWO

THE
ACT

paige press

CHARADE BOOK TWO

THE
ACT

STELLA GRAY

Paige Press
Leander, TX 78641

Ebook:
ISBN: 978-1-953520-40-1

Print:
ISBN: 978-1-953520-41-8

Editing: Erica Russikoff at Erica Edits
Proofing: Michele Ficht

Cruising through the halls of Wayland-Blaine Academy, there's not a doubt in my mind: I'm the king of the whole fucking school. It's unquestionable, irrefutable. Whatever I say, goes.

The guys respect me, offering head nods or salutes, and the girls want to fuck me, coyly lowering their lashes or flashing brazen, hungry grins. As a sophomore, it's a heady high knowing I command so much power already; I won't deny I take pleasure in wielding it. And at fifty grand a year in tuition, I'm ruling a lot more than just plebes in this place.

My subjects are the cream of the crop, the elite, the future leaders of America—or at least the city of Chicago— which means my influence will last a lot longer than the few years I'll spend in this place.

That said, the majority of the school's drama doesn't interest me. I don't care who's fucking who (unless, of course, it's one of the teachers) and I really don't care who's getting shit-talked or hang-wedgied in the bathroom. But a certain bullying incident has snowballed into an untenable situation, and I can't stop thinking about it.

The social destruction of Mara Zoric.

I'm not saying I'd never joined in on the abuse—everyone had—but at this point, enough was enough. It had gone too far. And I had my own reasons for taking issue with the whole thing.

If you were nice, you pitied the girl. If you weren't—and let's face it, most of my friends weren't—you mocked her to her face. She was the laughingstock of the whole school. I'd been in the locker room just this morning and seen her name and phone number written across the wall in big, fat sharpie, with "text for nudes" and "for a good time, call!" underneath it. Again.

Teenage boys had never much been known for their originality.

Not that the girls at this school were any better. One of them had used lipstick to write WHORE on her locker this morning.

Mara was taunted everywhere she went—the cafeteria, the gym, even the courtyard outside. It had started months ago, but things had been ramping up over the past few weeks for reasons unknown.

On the surface, nothing about her screamed "loser." She was on the short side, but she was pretty enough—big gray eyes, wide mouth, dark hair that was always hanging in her face—maybe a little mousy and awkward looking, sure, but nothing she wouldn't grow into eventually.

She also had these amazing tits, but she always wore a dark cardigan buttoned up over her uniform, as if that would help disguise them in any way. I could see why girls might be jealous. But I didn't get why the guys felt the need to drag the torture on and on so enthusiastically. Hadn't she been picked on enough?

I guess it just goes to show the enduring power of the high school rumor mill.

"Aww shit," Blake said. "Here she comes."

I stood with Blake and the rest of my friends, confident in my position at the top of the high school social hierarchy, and watched as the person occupying the rock-bottom of that hierarchy walked by, arms wrapped tightly around her books, chin tucked to her chest.

She looked pathetic, resigned to her sad fate. Truthfully, I felt sorry for her.

"Ho ho ho!" someone shouted at her.

I watched her flinch, but she just kept walking.

"There go the one-dollar blowjobs!" someone else yelled. "Get 'em while they're hot, under the bleachers!"

Mara tried to ignore them, but I could see her cheeks turning pink. It looked like she might cry. I hoped she wouldn't—tears would only make the teasing more aggressive.

A guy named Paul pushed off the wall as she came closer. I watched as he stepped right in her way.

"Hey Mara," he said.

She didn't say anything, her eyes fixed on the floor.

"Got a question for you," Paul went on.

No response.

"How much you charge for the Zoric special?" he asked. "I heard it's a good, cheap time."

Everyone burst into laughter as Mara pushed past him. I could see the tears welling up in her eyes but she was gone before they had a chance to fall.

I was a tiny bit impressed with that.

3

"Come on," I told Blake and the others as the bell rang. "We're gonna be late."

I didn't care much about being late, but I wasn't really interested in watching whatever Paul and the other high school idiots were going to do to Mara next.

She and I had study hall together. She walked into the library late that day.

When she arrived, I looked up just in time to see her walk past my table. Our eyes caught. Hers were red-rimmed. She'd managed to keep from crying in front of her tormentors, but she clearly hadn't managed to keep the tears completely at bay.

She looked away, hurrying to the study table she preferred in the back corner.

"There she goes," Blake said to me. "Pathetic."

He was drawing boobs in his notebook.

"Whatever," I said.

"Oh, come on," he said. "You don't think little Miss Russian Whore is pathetic?"

I just shrugged, not bothering to correct him—I knew for a fact that Mara and her older brothers were of Serbian descent, thanks to the genealogy project she'd presented in our history class last year. God, I was so bored with high school kids. So bored with all of this shit. I couldn't wait to graduate. To get out of this place. Out of my own house.

"I'm going to ask if she'll tutor me," Blake said, waggling his eyebrows. "Privately."

I rolled my eyes, hoping he was joking, but when he stood it was clear he intended to continue the teasing that Paul and the others had started in the hallway.

He strode to the back of the room. I watched.

"Hey Mara," he said.

She ignored him. Good girl.

"Mara Zoric. MZ. Em Zeeeee," he tried again, drawing out the last part of her name like a whine, drumming his hands on the stack of books beside her.

It was so annoying I wanted to punch him.

"What do you want?" she finally asked.

Blake put a hand to his chest, wearing an expression of comical hurt.

"Why the aggression? I was just trying to talk to you," he said.

Mara stared up at him. She wasn't stupid. She knew exactly what he was doing. We all did.

I glanced around and noticed that pretty much the whole room was watching the interaction from the corners of their eyes. The only person blatantly ignoring the harassment was the teacher in charge of study hall, a younger guy who spent the class period messing around on his smartphone, as if we couldn't see it under the table. It was obvious he didn't give a shit.

"I was just wondering..." Blake said, a shit-eating grin on his face. "If you offer discounts? You know, like two for one."

Mara's face went red and her eyes dropped back to the open textbook on the table.

It was almost adorable how innocent she was. At least, it might be adorable—if it wasn't for the fact that innocence got you absolutely nothing but abuse in this world.

"Come on," Blake coaxed. "I've seen the way you look at me. I know you want it. And I know I can get it for free anytime I want."

"Go away," she whispered, glancing over at the teacher who couldn't care less. Clearly, he wasn't going to save her.

"Don't be such a fucking tease," he said. "I'll even throw

in a ride from my good pal Ford over there. Come on, M, don't you want to see how the other half lives?"

As far as goading went, it was kind of weak. Especially because while Mara's family wasn't wealthy like mine was, they weren't close to poor either. No one at this school was.

"I'd give it to you so good," he went on. "Maybe you'd even pay me, you little slut."

"Please," Mara said, her voice grating a little. "Just stop."

It was the catch in her voice that got to me. How broken and desperate it was. He'd gone too far. Everyone had. That little mouse of a girl didn't deserve the kind of treatment she'd been getting, and I was sick of watching it play out like a TV rerun every fucking day.

As I stood, all eyes turned to me—including Mara's. There was apprehension in her gaze, and why wouldn't there be? I was the de facto king of the school. Whatever I said was law.

I walked over to her table.

"Right on, Malone," Blake said. "You ready to double team this bitch under the bleachers later?"

"I'm ready for you to leave her alone," I said coldly.

A murmur went through the room. Ford Malone standing up for Mara Zoric? It would be the gossip of the week.

"You serious?" Blake challenged, his grin starting to falter.

"Let it be," I told him, folding my arms over my broad chest. "I'm over this shit."

For a second, I thought he'd argue, but then he looked around. Everyone was watching.

"Whatever," he said, and walked back to our table. It was possible he'd be pissed and we'd fight about it later, but

I was half a foot taller and on the rowing team. I could handle him.

"You okay?" I asked Mara, even though I knew she wasn't. Not that I really cared.

But then she looked up at me, her eyes full of absolute adoration—and whatever guff I might take from my friends suddenly seemed totally worth it. Because as far as Mara Zoric was concerned, I had just become her hero.

EMZEE

CHAPTER 1

My wedding day had dawned like a dream, the New England skies a gorgeous blue and crystal clear, save for a few picturesque clouds. The sun was shining and the temperature was going to be mild. I couldn't have asked for better weather. Though I was pretty sure that if it hadn't cooperated, my sisters-in-law, through some sort of wedding magic, would have figured out a way to literally control the elements.

They had done absolutely everything in their power to make this the most perfect day a bride could hope for. Ford's family property on Martha's Vineyard was an exquisite venue for an outdoor ceremony. The rolling green lawn, impeccably manicured and shaded by mature trees, was the setting for almost six hundred cushioned chairs. They faced a dais that held a wedding arch draped in ivory chiffon, eucalyptus branches, and an actual crystal chandelier. Behind that was the sound, where deep blue water rocked rhythmically as sunlight glittered across its surface.

The end of each aisle was festooned with gigantic clusters of more eucalyptus branches, sprays of ferns, anemone blossoms in bright, bold shades, blue thistle, and classic ivory roses to match my luxurious bouquet. I'd asked for a mix of both rustic and traditional florals, and Brooklyn had knocked it out of the park. The red anemones matched her dress, and the blue ones matched Tori's. I was sure the color coordination wasn't an accident.

My dress, of course, was as perfect as the day I'd tried it on. *Every* detail was perfect. My sisters-in-law had truly outdone themselves, from the custom hand-done calligraphy on the invitations to the gourmet catering menu that I'd been thrilled to approve. Brooklyn had even taken Munchkin to the groomer's before bringing him on the flight out to the vineyard with her, so he'd be freshly spiffed up for the ceremony. I couldn't have dreamed up a better wedding.

But it was all pretend, and I was heartbroken.

The worst part was that I'd started to believe that it might not *have* to be pretend, and the way Ford had snuck into my dressing room to ask about my feelings had me wondering all over again if this sham could have been real after all.

What would have happened if I had just told him the truth? That I *did* love him?

No. It wasn't even worth considering. The wedding— the marriage—had to be a lie. All of it. Ford could never know how I really felt.

If I told him the truth, there would be no rescue for my family, nor for our business. The Malones had only promised to bail out Danica Rose Management from its entanglement with the Russian mob as long as I agreed to walk out on this marriage in a year's time. I couldn't sacrifice the entire Zoric family—my brothers, their wives, their children, their livelihoods and legacies—for my own selfish ends. My own feelings.

After the agency's debt was paid off and my divorce was finalized, I had no idea what would happen between me and Ford. Maybe our friendship of seven-plus years could be salvaged. Maybe not. But right now, I couldn't let myself think about that. I needed all my focus, all my strength, to get me through this farce of a wedding. The worst best day of my life.

"Are you ready?" Stefan asked me.

Startled out of my thoughts, I forced a smile as I heard the bridal waltz begin. I was waiting in a tent that had been set up specifically for the purpose of hiding me from the guests—and the groom—but once I walked out onto the grass, there would be no turning back.

"I am," I said, lifting my chin resolutely. "Thank you for doing this."

Since my father was a monster and very much behind bars, I had asked my oldest brother to give me away. Stefan stood there in his suit, elbow crooked for me to take, smiling down at me with a softness in his eyes that I rarely ever saw.

"Hey," I said. "Remember when you took me to your senior prom because I was a total loser freshman with no friends, and after that, the entire school knew my name?"

He grinned. "Yeah."

"This kind of feels like that. Like you're presenting me to the world or something."

Cocking a brow, he said, "Meaning you're nervous as hell and you want me to be your first dance?"

"Totally."

Stefan nodded. "Done. And seriously, don't be nervous. The only thing that matters today is that you're here with Ford, starting your new life together. Just focus on that."

Except focusing on that was the whole problem, wasn't it? Because the only thing Ford and I were starting together was a twelve-month lie.

Still, Stefan's words warmed me. No matter what happened with my marriage, I knew my family had my back. That would have to be enough.

I looped my right arm through Stefan's left, and off we marched down the aisle. Hundreds of our friends and family—mostly Ford's—watched as we approached. Whispers reached my ears, and I felt the weight of all those eyes on me, ratcheting up my anxiety. My bouquet started shaking in my grip.

God, what was I doing? Was this all a huge mistake?

But then I felt Stefan's strong hand gently close over mine, steadying the bouquet.

"Just look straight ahead," he whispered.

And I did.

The second I saw Ford standing under the arch, everything else disappeared. I knew him well enough to recognize that the smile he wore was fake, but I couldn't tear my eyes away.

Suddenly, I realized we'd reached the dais. Stefan kissed my cheek as we walked up the steps, whispering, "You got this," and then he passed my hand to Ford.

To the left and right, I saw Tori and Brooklyn, Luka and Stefan, and Ford's handful of groomsmen and groomswomen, everyone wearing vibrant spring colors of their own choosing just as I'd requested. Even Munchkin was wearing a little Liberty floral doggie bow tie, with Brooklyn holding his matching leash. Everyone looked fabulous, like something straight out of a bridal magazine. Me, on the other hand? I had to be the world's most miserable bride at the world's most beautiful wedding.

I glanced up at Ford, but his expression was so stoic and inscrutable that it felt like we were two strangers standing up there together, rather than longtime best friends who were about to commit ourselves to each other. Nothing about this felt right.

"It is my great honor to welcome everyone to the wedding of Mara Zoric and Ford Malone," the officiant began.

Time sped up as the ceremony proceeded, just like everyone had warned me it would. I was glad. When we were instructed to recite our vows, I kept imagining how they might sound if they were factual.

"Do you, Ford, take Mara to be your protection against your shitty ex-girlfriend Claudia and your family's pathological desire for you to marry and knock up someone of their choosing? And do you, Mara, take Ford as your way to bail your family out of yet another treacherous hole your criminal father dug, this time with the Russian mafia?"

It was almost comical. But I didn't feel like laughing.

Of course, I said nothing, reciting my marital vows with as much feeling as I could muster even though it felt like I was dying inside.

"It is my pleasure to declare you husband and wife," the officiant said jovially. "Ford, you may now kiss the bride."

The kiss, though.

I'd expected it to be as polite and perfunctory as Ford's responses had been during the rest of the ceremony. Instead, he pulled me into his arms so fast that I barely had a chance to register the intensity in his gaze before his mouth came down on mine.

The kiss was incendiary. It was indecent. It was furious, possessive, and fucking hot.

No matter what was happening between us, no matter

what lies I'd told, I couldn't hide my feelings in that kiss—
and it was impossible to deny that our chemistry was still
there, as fierce as ever. It was the kind of chemistry that
might burn down the big, red barn on the other side of the
property where we would be holding the reception. Trying
to deny it was a burden that was taking all my strength.

So for one, perfect, blissful moment, I forgot everything.
I forgot about the lies. I forgot about the deals. Hell, I even
forgot that we were in the middle of our actual wedding and
probably giving Ford's grandmother (and the rest of the
Malones) one hell of a show. Ford's lips against mine were
like a spark to kindling. He held me tightly against him, his
body hard against mine. I wanted him. I wanted him so bad.

When we finally broke apart, we were both breathing
heavily. Brooklyn let out an ear-piercing whistle, Munchkin
started yapping, and people were applauding. It almost
seemed as though Ford had been trying to prove something
with that kiss, though I wasn't sure what.

He took my hand and we made our way back down the
aisle, now officially married. Our guests cheered, but as I
passed Ford's parents, I saw absolutely nothing in their
expression to indicate they were celebrating this union. In
fact, I would have bet anything that they were already
counting down the days until I was gone so they could bring
Claudia back into the fold.

Somehow, I made it through the rest of the festivities.

Like the ceremony, everything was perfect. Not that I
could enjoy it. It was especially hard because I had to
pretend two different things—to Ford, that I only had
friendly feelings for him; to everyone else, that I was a
blissful bride. It didn't matter how many dances I danced,
how many bites of lobster dipped in melted butter that I let
Ford feed me, how beautiful our exotic orchid-covered

Belgian chocolate cake was. I was purely going through the motions. The joy of the day couldn't touch me.

All I wanted was for the day to be over, and I felt unbearably guilty about it. Tori and Brooklyn had put so much love into planning every little thing down to the last detail, and not only could I not enjoy it, I was actively wishing for it to end.

Finally, after what felt like ages, the reception started winding down. I was utterly exhausted from pretending. My face hurt from all the forced smiling. I just wanted to escape.

Unfortunately we were leaving for St. Barts in a couple of hours. Off on a honeymoon that I'd legitimately been looking forward to a couple of days ago. Before Ford's parents had sprung their deal on me, I'd been hoping the time away from our real lives—away from the stresses of Danica Rose's debt to the Bratva and Ford's family obligations—might give my new faux husband a chance to realize that our fake marriage could potentially be something more.

Now, it just seemed like another fresh form of torture. The two of us, alone on a tropical island, sharing a luxurious suite at a romantic resort? How would I be able to survive it?

Hand in hand, Ford and I went up to our room to finish getting ready for the trip. His family's private jet had been chartered to fly us from the Vineyard to the more accessible airport on the island of St. Martin, and from there we'd take a forty-minute ferry ride over to St. Barts. I'd read that the water could be choppy, so I was praying for smooth sailing.

As I packed up my suitcase, I could tell by the look in his eyes that he was interested in finishing what he started on the dais, in front of our guests. But I couldn't allow that to happen. There could be no sex tonight. I had to be strong.

Luggage zipped and ready to go, I stretched and yawned as dramatically as possible.

"I'm beat," I told Ford drowsily. "I need to take a nap before we leave. The car's picking us up in what, five hours?"

Then, before he could respond, I went into the bathroom to take a quick shower, locking the door behind me. It was cowardly, I knew that...but I also knew that if Ford kissed me like he had earlier, I wouldn't be able to say no. The problem wasn't that I didn't want him. It was that I wanted him *too* much.

And after an entire day of pretending, I knew that if he took me in his arms, I wouldn't be able to keep it up.

EMZEE

CHAPTER 2

At just over nine and a half square miles, St. Barts was definitely the tiniest tropical island I'd ever visited. I also suspected it might turn out to be the ritziest, considering that the French West Indies territory was referred to as the Hamptons of the Caribbean. But the minute I laid eyes on the picturesque, red-roofed capital city of Gustavia from the ferry, I was enchanted.

"Wow," I murmured, not realizing I'd spoken out loud until Ford looked over.

It was the first time he'd torn his gaze from his phone since we'd gotten on the boat almost an hour ago. "You like?" he asked, gesturing at the curved expanse of beach.

"I *love*," I answered.

Falling for St. Barts was easy. The teal blue water, the quaint buildings huddled along the palm tree dotted shore, the lush hills, dense with greenery, the white sand—the whole place looked like paradise.

Sure, my family had gone to a fancy resort in the Bahamas for Luka's birthday last year, and of course I'd been to the beaches of Florida and to Cancun for Spring

Break...but this was something else. It wasn't overrun with tourists or neon signs or souvenir shops, and seemed like more of a low-key hideaway than a party town. I felt like I had truly left the stress of my life behind and arrived someplace utterly charming and magical. Even Ford seemed to be affected by the magic; when I squeezed his hand, he squeezed right back.

When we stepped off the ferry, a uniformed man from our hotel was waiting for us with a wheeled luggage trolley and a grin.

"Mr. and Mrs. Malone?" he asked, holding up a sign with our names on it. "Welcome to St. Barts. I'm Phillipe, your dedicated concierge, courtesy of Eden Rock. I'll be taking care of all your needs during your stay—twenty-four/seven. Please allow me to chauffeur you to your accommodations."

We were staying in a private villa at a luxurious boutique resort, and Eden Rock more than lived up to its name. The hotel was practically on its own island, most of it jutting out over the crystal clear water, with a mossy-looking garden of coral just below the cliffs.

The modern-style villa Phillipe brought us to was stunning. High ceilings, light-filled rooms, teak wood and crisp white fabric everywhere, and panoramic windows providing an unobstructed view of St. Jean beach and its azure waters. The windows gave the impression that our villa was floating over the ocean, and someone had thoughtfully placed fresh flowers throughout the house. Outside, the property had a deck with an infinity pool, a fire pit, a bar, woven hammocks and umbrella-shaded loungers, and our own personal palm trees. My God.

It was gorgeous, and so chic that I immediately felt self-conscious about my worn black leggings and rumpled appearance after the four-hour flight and slightly nauseating ferry ride.

"I set up your private cabana on the beach this morning," Phillipe informed us, "so please let me know if you'd like an escort there or anywhere else. You also have a dedicated chef on call, your own butler, and, of course, the entire Eden Rock Guestcare team at your service."

"This is incredible," I breathed. "Thank you so much."

"You're very welcome, Mrs. Malone. And congratulations to both of you on your recent nuptials. We're happy to do everything possible to ensure your honeymoon with us exceeds your expectations in every regard."

Ford thanked him again, discreetly pressing a folded bill into the man's palm before sending him away. Then he turned to me.

"How are you feeling? Up for an adventure?"

Even though I was dog tired after what had seemed like an endless day of pretend-wedding followed by hours of travel, I wanted to explore. It was still daytime, and I didn't want to waste a single moment of our time on the island.

"Hell yes," I answered. "I just need to change clothes. What do you want to do?"

"Let's go to the beach," he said.

I smiled. "Perfect. I'll put my suit on."

It was the most we'd spoken to each other since leaving Martha's Vineyard. Things still felt chilly between us, but they were starting to thaw. Maybe we could treat this trip like a friendly vacation after all.

As I ducked into the bathroom to change into my Agent Provocateur one-piece (black, of course), I couldn't help feeling a little ridiculous. Ford had seen me naked plenty of times in the weeks leading up to the wedding. But I couldn't risk what might happen if he saw me naked. If I saw the look in his eyes as he watched me change. I wouldn't be able to resist him.

Obviously this whole avoiding-sex thing couldn't go on forever—we were married and it was inevitable—but I still felt too vulnerable, too worn down from the emotional roller coaster of the last few days. It was pointless to think about that now, though.

The deal had been made. Now I had to follow through with it.

I pulled my hair back and threw on a patterned DVF cover-up dress—my sexy swimsuit had seemed like a perfect choice when I'd gone shopping with Tori and Brooklyn for my honeymoon, but now I just felt exposed. In fact, my entire suitcase was stuffed with sexy nothings, from lingerie to dresses to bathing suits. The black suit I was wearing technically covered everything, but looked held together with string. Still, it was the most modest one I had.

Cursing my past self for being so naïvely romantic and optimistic, I headed back out to the living room and told Ford I was ready. He was in nothing but swim trunks and sandals, and it took all my willpower not to drool all over myself at the sight of his already perfectly tanned, tight-abbed torso.

"Do you, umm, want to call Phillipe?" I asked. "To take us to the cabana?"

Ford shook his head. "Nah. We can do the cabana later. I just want to stroll for now."

"Okay. Great." But it wasn't great.

At the cabana, I could read a book, drink a margarita, take a nap in my own chaise lounge a safe distance away from my half-naked, sexy-as-fuck new husband. Walking with Ford, though, there'd be nothing to keep me from clinging to his hand, feeling the warmth of his body next to mine, breathing him in, dreaming about throwing him down on the sand and climbing him like a tree. It would be torture.

We headed down to St. Jean's, and from the sand I picked out a few kayaks and small yachts in the water, some windsurfers, boats taking people to snorkel. The boats were close enough that I could see more than one couple huddled against the rails together as they headed to where there was probably a gorgeous coral reef full of sea life. For a brief moment, I imagined Ford and me out there, just another happily married new couple on their honeymoon.

He'd make some raunchy joke about my snorkel, I'd hit him in the arm. He'd pretend to be a shark or something, tickling my feet while we were swimming around, I'd get back at him by putting my hand over the top of his snorkel. We'd steal kisses in the waves and climb out of the boat, wet and salty and hungry. But not for food. We'd rush back to our room, not even bothering to fully remove our swimsuits before he'd be fucking me against the door.

"Sunscreen?" Ford asked, breaking my reverie.

"What?" I'd barely heard him.

"You don't want to burn up on your first day."

"Right. Sure," I said, digging around in my beach bag for the spray can of SPF 45 I'd picked up at the airport in St. Martin while Ford had been off exchanging dollars for Euros.

"Here, I'll do it."

He knelt and started spraying me, ankle to thigh, shoulder to wrist, my back and neck, stroking my bare skin in slow circles after each spray to rub it in. Standing still the whole time he massaged me under the thin fabric of my dress was a challenge, as was holding in my moans. I could feel myself getting wet. If I didn't know any better, I'd think he was trying to seduce me right there on the beach.

Luckily, I was able to hide my blush beneath the wide brim of my straw sun hat.

We walked along the postcard-perfect beach, Ford pointing out the church built in 1855 and the lighthouse, as well as a few of the huge, free-roaming iguanas I'd read about. I couldn't help wishing that we were actually *enjoying* the snorkeling and windsurfing going on all around us, rather than me spending my time with Ford secretly fantasizing about what could have been.

Since picnics were more common than restaurants that were open for lunch, we stopped at a small grocery store and bought a few things, packing a mix of cheeses, fruit, fresh bread, cold cuts, water, and wine into my beach bag for later.

"I have an idea," Ford said, turning to me as we exited the shop.

Much to my surprise, he had a mischievous grin on his face. He'd barely smiled—really smiled—for most of the day. It was almost jarring to see it now.

"What kind of idea?"

He grabbed my hand. "Come on."

Having no idea where this was all leading, I decided it would just be easier to go along with it than try to make sense of Ford's changing mood.

It was a decision I regretted the moment we arrived at the Anse Grande Saline.

A nude beach.

"What do you think?" he asked, still wearing that grin.

I was speechless.

All around us were naked people. I wasn't a prude, and I'd been to a nude beach or two on various vacations, but this felt totally different. Mainly because I was with Ford. The person I was trying desperately not to be in love—or lust—with.

But he had just laid out a blanket for us under the shade of a few palms, and was already stripping down to his birthday suit. There was no turning back.

His thumbs hooked into the waistband of his swim trunks, and I watched—rapt—as with one smooth movement, he whisked them away, exposing his hard, gorgeous body in its entirety. I was probably imagining it, but I was certain I could hear the sound of the entire female population on the beach letting out a sigh of appreciation.

Part of me wanted to throw my hands over him and shout, "Mine!"

The other part of me wanted to do whatever I could to avoid any kind of attention at all.

Ford didn't seem to have that problem. He looked amazing and he knew it. And yeah, I had to admit that his flawless body was worth a few fantasies of its own. With his hands on his hips, he faced the ocean, looking like a Greek god in the sunlight. My mouth went dry at the sight of him, and because he wasn't looking at me, I could stare at him as much as I wanted.

Nothing that had happened over the last few days had tamed my desire for him. Not one iota. Especially now that I had personally experienced the full scope of what his body could do.

Turning around, his hot gaze swept over me.

"You're not going to keep that on, are you?" he asked.

I was still wearing my beach dress and my swimsuit. Compared to everyone else, I looked like I was practically in formal wear.

Taking my clothes off was the last thing I wanted to do,

but people were starting to stare. Staying fully dressed was obviously drawing far more attention than being naked would.

Ford was watching me expectantly, a smile playing at the corners of his mouth.

"Just a minute," I said, feeling flustered.

I took off my hat first, dropping it onto the towel, and then loosened the ties of my dress and unwrapped it. Trying to ignore Ford's eyes following my every movement, I slid down one strap of my swimsuit and then the other. But then I looked up, and our eyes locked. With all the heat in his gaze, I completely forgot that we were on a crowded beach and I was about to do a striptease for a hundred strangers. I pushed my swimsuit down, exposing my breasts.

I knew that Ford liked my breasts. Licking his lips, sending a shockwave of want through me, his gaze moved down and continued to follow the path of my swimsuit as I tugged it over my hips, past my narrow landing strip, down my thighs, and then let it drop to the sand.

I swallowed hard, wondering what he would do next. I half expected him to throw me over his shoulder and run all the way back to the hotel. But when he looked at me again, he was suddenly the same man who had been waiting for me at the end of the aisle earlier that day. His face was impassive. Cool. Impossible to read.

"I'm going for a swim," he said.

"Me too," I said, but he was already striding toward the water, turning heads as he did.

Feeling more naked than I had when I first got undressed, I followed, wanting to hide.

The water was crystal clear, which didn't provide much cover, but I still felt better when I dove in. The ocean was warm and perfect. I felt the weight of the day lift off my shoulders as I swam into the softly cresting waves. Ford stayed nearby, diving under and reemerging farther out with a toss of his head that flicked a cascade of water into the air.

I took a break to put on more sunscreen and have a snack, watching Ford swim. When he realized I'd gone back to our towel, I held up the bottle of wine to lure him over, but he just tapped his wrist as if to say "in a few minutes," and by the time he got out of the water, I was ready to get back in. Or I guess, ready to avoid the possibility of us sitting on a towel naked and wet together. It was too tempting.

We stayed until late afternoon. Making my way over the sand toward our shady spot, I pulled my hair over my shoulder to squeeze the water out of it, savoring the delicious exhaustion coursing through me after hours of sun and swimming. I had just dropped to my knees on the edge of the towel when strong arms lifted me up, and I found myself gazing at Ford.

"What are you—" I began, wondering if he was about to kiss me.

"Centipedes," he said, and I looked down and realized that he wasn't being romantic at all. Instead, he'd just rescued me from stretching my naked self out on top of a couple of the island's native black and red bugs that had made themselves at home in the folds of the towel. I'd heard they were venomous, but I hadn't been prepared for how gigantic they were.

Shuddering in his arms, I said, "Fuck. You're my hero."

Ford's expression went shuttered and distant right before my eyes. "Don't mention it."

He set me down and helped me shake out my clothes so I could get dressed. Then he checked inside the beach bag

25

to be sure we weren't inadvertently taking any of the critters with us before heading back to our villa.

After a long day of waiting to assist us, Phillipe was thrilled to make a reservation for us at the Eden Rock's Sand Restaurant. The place had a relaxed, luxurious vibe and a decadent menu, but Ford and I were so tired that we agreed to make it a quick meal and go to bed early.

Being the resident foodie, I expected to get more pleasure out of the local mahi-mahi and coconut sorbet I ordered, but between the physical exhaustion of the day and the emotional strain of holding myself back around my new husband, I barely tasted anything.

After a quick shower back at the villa, I crawled into bed beside Ford, expecting to pass out the second my head hit the pillow. But he surprised me by rolling over and taking me in his arms.

His kiss was sweet, but it felt more obligatory than romantic—it couldn't hold a candle to the kiss at the wedding. Still, my body began to respond almost instantly, and when he rolled the condom on, I was ready for him. He kissed me as he fucked me, and we both came without too much effort...but once we were finished, I couldn't help feeling like the first post-wedding sex I'd had with my husband had been decent but perfunctory. Like we'd both been on autopilot.

It was disappointing, even though I knew a lot of that was on me.

The moment I'd decided to take the Malones' bribe and lie to Ford about my feelings, everything between us had shifted. Even still, I couldn't seem to stop myself from hoping that Ford would make some sort of gesture. Shout his love from the rooftops, so I could shout mine back.

Maybe then we could join forces and find a way out of this mess together.

But as I drifted off, I realized that even a fairy tale gesture could never fix the web of mistakes and dishonesty we'd gotten ourselves tangled up in.

FORD

CHAPTER 3

I'd made my decision. It was time to handle this.

For some unknowable reason, the dynamic between me and Emzee had undergone a complete one-eighty over the last few days, and I hated it. Our honeymoon—our relationship—couldn't go on like this. Even the sex, which had always been scorching hot, had changed.

Emzee was still sleeping, but I had woken up early, brain in turmoil.

Now, as I paced the living room of our luxurious villa, all I could think about was finding a solution for our problem.

I tried to convince myself that this new awkwardness had nothing to do with her saying she didn't love me. Which was fine. Hell, I'd never expected to marry for love. I was pretty sure I didn't even believe in the concept. After all, what was love anyway, other than basic affection combined with dopamine and oxytocin (which declined over time, according to science)?

And look at the example I'd grown up with. My parents clearly didn't love each other, and they'd made it work. For over two decades and still going strong, or whatever adjective you'd use to describe their marriage. It didn't seem to be a union of convenience, per se, but it was certainly symbiotic. Maybe their bond had more to do with their compatible social and economic status, but they both seemed fine with that. I could be fine with that.

But...something was missing between me and Em. Something that used to be there. And I wanted it back.

I wanted the Emzee who seemed to be falling for me, who delighted in sharing in my adventures as well as savoring quiet cups of coffee and comfortable silences while Munchkin snoozed between us on the couch. The snarky, witty, down-for-whatever Emzee.

I wanted the Emzee whose big, sparkling laugh surprised me every time it came out of her usually serious little body. It was a reminder that no matter how much of an overthinker she tended to be, she could also roll with the punches. In fact, now that I thought about it, I realized she *thrived* in unexpected situations and moments of crisis.

It occurred to me that this strength might actually be the silver lining to her family life being so off-kilter. Not just recently, either. It had always been that way.

Growing up, she'd had to constantly adjust to her father's ever-expanding list of demands and expectations; I'd heard plenty of stories about how she'd been sent to etiquette lessons as a child, trained to speak and act a certain way, all kinds of pressure heaped on her small shoulders and made even more overwhelming thanks to the fact that her mom had died when she was a baby and her father was chronically absent—running his criminal empire, no doubt, though of course she hadn't known that at the time.

But just look at how beautifully she performed under pressure now. Case in point, when I had sprung this fake relationship—and then a surprise engagement—on her. Every time, she'd played along in front of friends and family without batting an eye. To the point that she almost had *me* fooled into thinking she loved me right before our fake wedding.

Almost.

It was obvious that her confidence blossomed whenever she took on new roles. Sure, she might be hesitant at first, but more often than not, I would bet she even surprised *herself* to find how capable she was. It was like the stress brought out a completely different side of her. She just needed a challenge to rise to.

Huh.

Maybe I'd just found the answer to my problem.

Sinking onto the cloud-like cushions of the couch, I grabbed the complimentary island guidebook off the coffee table and started flipping through it, hoping for inspiration.

I found it under the "Hotel Activities" section.

Windsurfing.

Phillipe was more than happy to make arrangements for us, and I also had him place an order for a hot breakfast to be brought to our villa right away.

Then I woke Emzee up. Her innocent eyes blinked at me drowsily as I told her the plan.

"I don't know anything about windsurfing," she said.

"Me neither," I said. "We'll fumble through it together. And if we fail, we'll fail spectacularly. Phillipe already reserved us a spot, and he's meeting us in the lobby after we eat."

"Eat what?" she asked, suddenly a whole lot more awake.

My little foodie. "It's a surprise," I said. "I requested a hot breakfast for two."

Having your own personal, round-the-clock concierge, it turned out, was not too shabby at all. The cart that arrived while we were getting showered and dressed held a pot of strong coffee, a carafe of fresh-squeezed orange juice, savory prosciutto and Gruyère cheese crepes, sliced mango, and a side of poached eggs. It was the perfect combination of light and filling to get us ready for the day's activities.

As we headed to the hotel lobby, swimsuits under our clothes, I couldn't help staring at Emzee's hips and ass as she walked in front of me. She'd nearly killed me with that fucking striptease the other day. I thought I'd been so clever taking us to a nude beach, but I hadn't considered how it might backfire. And backfire it had.

Her sexy black suit was bad enough—it didn't reveal anything, but it didn't cover much either. It was like a basic black one-piece that had been shredded by Wolverine, clinging to Emzee's mouthwatering curves so good that it had taken all the baseball statistics I knew—reciting them over and over in my head—in order to keep from completely embarrassing myself on a public nude beach with a massive hard-on for my wife.

I'd just about had it under control, but then Emzee tossed her hat on the towel and began the longest, most agonizing striptease I'd ever seen in my life. Watching her flash those perfect, lush tits before sliding the suit down to expose the rest of her tight, mouthwatering body to the St. Barts sunlight (and the hungry gaze of every red-blooded male in the vicinity), had put a fire inside of me that I had barely been able to contain.

So I had done the only thing I could. I turned away from the sight of my gorgeous, naked wife and walked right into the ocean. It had been too warm to completely cool my ardor, but at least it had hidden my erection when Em joined me, the clear blue water sluicing over her curves as she dove into the waves.

In the end, all I had to do to keep from flashing an erection was think about Emzee's flat, emotionless expression on our wedding day when she said she didn't love me. That killed off my desire pretty quickly, and it didn't resurface again until later that night. Still, when I turned to her in bed, I could sense that she was holding herself back a little. So was I.

Still, the sex was good. It was never not good with Em; our physical attraction was too strong. I made her come pretty fast, could feel the contractions of her cunt squeezing me hard enough that I knew she wasn't faking her orgasm, but things still felt off. I thought about how I had surprised her in the dressing room at the wedding dress shop, how responsive and hot she had been, especially knowing we could get caught at any moment.

That's why this whole windsurfing thing was such a great idea. We just needed to bond over new, daring experiences. It had always been a vital component of our friendship.

Phillipe dropped us off at the beach where he'd reserved our private lesson, so it was just me, Emzee, and the instructor. I was grateful it was an older woman, not one of the young cabana boys that seemed to constantly be running around in their flashy little Speedos.

Our instructor Angie walked us through the basics while we were still on the beach.

"First things first, we need to know which direction the wind is coming from." She held up a finger, motioning for us to do the same, and then pointed. "I happen to know the wind forecast for today is seventeen knots from the northeast, which is actually perfect for a first-timer. It's your lucky day!"

"Good to hear it," I said. I felt like I was overdue a bit of luck.

"When you launch your board into the water," Angie went on, "you'll want to make sure your back and the mast are facing the wind. Otherwise you'll never get your sail up."

"So...we'll be walking into the water backwards?" Emzee asked.

"For today, yes." Angie nodded as she carried on with her introductory information.

I glanced over at Em, who was listening so intently I was surprised she hadn't pulled a notebook and pen out of her bag to take notes. Meanwhile, Angie was explaining how to use the direction of the sail to steer the board once we were out on the water, throwing around terms like uphaul and daggerboard and boom so fast I could barely keep up.

I'd always been a natural when it came to any kind of sport, but since I was new to windsurfing, I did my best to focus more on the lesson and less on Emzee. It wasn't easy.

"When you pull the sail up out of the water, you want to keep your back straight," Angie said, hopping on the board resting in the sand to show us how it was done. "Use your leg strength to lift, not your back."

Emzee nodded. "Legs, not back," she repeated obediently.

It was kind of adorable how she was so intent on getting this right immediately. Me, I learned by doing. And I always did things well.

Angie instructed Em to get on the board to practice the

proper sail-lifting and boom-holding techniques she'd need once we were actually on the water.

"Cross one hand over the other to grab the boom," Angie said, "and then you'll use the boom to turn the sail and fill it with power."

Fill the sail with power. I could get into that.

Coming up behind Emzee, I wrapped my arms around hers so we could go through the motions of steering together. Angie looked on approvingly, stopping us every now and again to adjust or explain. After another twenty minutes of demonstrating rig steering, tacking, and jibing, she finally announced that we were ready to surf.

"Here goes nothin'," I said, grinning at Emzee. I was more than ready to hit the waves and see what the fuss was all about.

"I'm nervous," she said. "What if I wipe out?"

"The board stops the second the sail hits the water, so it won't go anywhere until you get back on," I reminded her. "But who cares if you fall? We're just here to have fun."

She nodded, still looking all kinds of serious. "Okay."

Reaching over, I cupped her face in my hands and kissed the little stress line between her brows, which always appeared when she was anxious. When I pulled away, she looked calmer.

"Let's do this," I said.

The water was perfect, clear as crystal and warm from the sun. I enjoyed the work required to get my board in the water, enjoyed moving my body and feeling my muscles respond. The last few weeks I'd been completely focused on the wedding and family stuff, and hadn't been able to get even a moment alone to just breathe. For the first time since this whole charade had begun, I felt like I was in control of myself again.

I watched Emzee get on her board first. I could see her hesitate, but then she clenched her jaw, squared her shoulders, and pulled the sail up out of the water like an absolute pro.

"Bravo," Angie shouted, clapping for Em.

When I managed to do the same, I didn't get the same standing ovation. Guess Angie had a favorite, and it wasn't me. Not that it mattered. The excitement on Emzee's face was the whole reason we were doing this in the first place.

As our boards moved through the water, slowly at first, I found myself thinking the whole thing was a little anticlimactic. We were on the ocean, sure, and it was beautiful—but nothing special. Then, all of a sudden, the wind picked up, filling our sails with the power we'd been promised. And just like that, we were off.

It was pure magic.

We were sailing along so fast it was like flying, the wind in our faces as we skimmed the waves, boards bouncing up and down. It was exhilarating and I couldn't get enough.

My muscles ached as I got used to the way I needed to hold the boom, the way I needed to plant my feet. I was grateful for the hours I put in every week at the gym, but I knew my entire body would be sore tomorrow regardless. At the moment, though, I didn't care.

All that mattered to me was the wind, the ocean, and my wife.

Emzee was up ahead of me, dark hair streaming behind her as she maneuvered her board. The water sprayed up around her as she moved toward the choppier waves, following Angie's lead as she took us farther out. I tasted salt, from the ocean and the air, feeling completely alive as we glided across the water.

And then I watched as Emzee faltered and almost took

a spill, her board swerving as she struggled to regain control over it. For a moment, I thought her earlier fears would be confirmed, that she'd crash right into the water with a big splash, but at the last minute she righted herself, letting out a girlish shriek of relief and pure delight before dissolving into giggles.

Emzee laughing about her near-fall was the exact thing I'd been missing, and it was impossible not to laugh with her. She glanced back at me, and the expression of joy I saw in her smile made my heart twist. I wanted to live in this moment with her forever.

Suddenly, I understood why that combination of affection and dopamine inspired poets and musicians to immortalize it.

But like the fathomless ocean beneath us, I knew, love was just as fraught with danger.

EMZEE

CHAPTER 4

W ho would have ever thought I'd have such an instant love affair with windsurfing?

When Ford had first woken me up to tell me it was our activity for the day, I'd been anxious. The honeymoon activities I'd been dreaming of consisted of going out to eat at the fanciest restaurants, snorkeling in the shallows, and maybe booking a couple's massage. Stuff that was more relaxing than athletic.

But windsurfing was more amazing than I could have imagined.

It definitely wasn't the type of activity I would have done on my own, but Ford had been so into it that I couldn't turn him down—and wasn't that what I'd always loved most about him? That he pushed me to try new things? And thank God he had.

Even though I'd paid more attention during the lesson, Ford had more natural skill and strength. After our official instruction was over, our teacher—a warm, older woman with box braids named Angie—left us to our own devices.

Yes, I had expected it to be challenging and scary. But I

hadn't expected it to be so fun. So thrilling. So...freeing. I could have stayed out on the water until the sun went down. Unfortunately, my growling stomach had other ideas, so we'd given our concierge a call and arranged for a ride back to our private villa. We still had yet to figure out dinner plans.

As I dried off after my shower, all I could think about was how blissful the day had been. It was almost romantic the way Ford had helped me learn during our lesson with Angie, coming up behind me on the beach while I stood on the board so he could wrap his arms around me and help me practice steering the sail. In fact, with all the touching and closeness of the past few hours, my guard was fully down. Which was why I was hoping for a quiet night in, since that meant there'd be less of a chance of me doing something I would regret...like giving in to the simmering sexual tension that had been building ever since Ford put his arms around me earlier.

After hours out on the ocean, I expected him to suggest giving the concierge a call to put in an order with our personal chef for dinner at home. But when I walked back out to the living room, I saw that he'd changed into a crisp linen shirt and slacks, his hair freshly combed and his eyes bright. The scent of his cologne wafted over, and the urge to throw myself at him increased.

"You look nice. Got a hot date?" I asked teasingly.

"I want to take you out," Ford said.

I felt a low tug in my belly, and a smile played at my lips. "Where to?"

"It's a surprise," he said.

"Hmmm..." I deliberated. "Does this surprise include dinner?"

"Indeed it does," Ford said with a grin. "And I know how much you love sushi."

"Done," I said. "Just let me put on something nicer than sweatpants. Give me a minute."

So much for that quiet night in, but I was still buzzing and exuberant from our day out on the ocean. And how could I insist on calling it a night when every part of me wanted to keep up the good vibes we'd built back up between us? Sure I was exhausted, but this was my honeymoon. Fake or not, I should take advantage of it. Especially if good sushi was involved.

I whipped off my loungewear and changed into one of the many beautiful dresses I'd brought with me, which was a rich shade of teal, short and tight and totally not my usual style. While shopping for this trip, Tori and Brooklyn had insisted I buy a few things that were outside the box for me.

"You can't wear all black on the beach in St. Barts," Tori had said. "You'll roast."

"Plus you need to mix it up a bit," Brooklyn had said. "Surprise yourself."

"Surprise Ford!" Tori had added and the two of them had giggled.

I'd taken their advice and picked out several flashy little dresses in actual colors, dresses that could be worn to a nice restaurant or out to a club depending on how I accessorized. The one I had on sported a deep neckline and no sleeves. I paired it with strappy heeled sandals and my favorite gold bangle, then tugged my hair out of its ponytail and shook it out into damp waves. I didn't do too much with my makeup, just a simple smoky eye and clear gloss over my lips.

When I came out of the bathroom, Ford's gaze swept appreciatively over my body.

"You look good enough to eat," he said, his voice husky.

Then he cleared his throat, as if snapping himself out of his lust trance. "You ready?"

"Ready," I said, feeling myself blushing.

I didn't know how much longer I could resist him—or if I even still wanted to.

The place Ford chose was one of the island's most prestigious bars, a harborside night club with live music and, he swore, a killer sushi and tapas bar at its center. Walking through the doors, I could tell instantly that it was *the* place to be in St. Barts.

It was an intimate venue, crowded with an eclectic array of beautiful people dancing to the Caribbean jazz, drinking brightly colored cocktails, and having a great time. I knew the island was a haven for the rich and famous, so it wasn't a surprise to see what looked like a few models and a young male pop star amidst the revelers, a mix of locals and tourists. Warm red lighting gave the ambiance a sensual haze. It matched how I was already feeling.

Once we were seated at the bar, I was dazzled by the array of options on the menu. Windsurfing had given me an insane appetite, but I couldn't decide on anything.

"What'll it be?" Ford asked.

"Gah! I want it all," I blurted.

"We can swing that," he said with a laugh, motioning over a waiter and telling him to bring us a sushi boat for two.

"An entire *boat* full of sushi?" I gasped.

"It's a small boat," Ford said, a gleam in his eye. "I'm sure you can handle it."

As we downed our first course of hot miso soup, I tried not to stare at my husband. He just looked so delicious in his crisp white shirt, and my stomach did this little flip whenever I glanced over at him. Occasionally, our eyes would meet, and I'd feel the heat from his gaze spread through my entire body. It was impossible not to blush, though I was certain he couldn't tell in the red light of the bar.

And then the boat arrived.

Hot damn.

The huge platter was oblong and held a selection of sushi, sashimi, maki, and seaweed. Salmon, yellowfin tuna, mahi, smoked eel (I'd been late to the eel party, but once I'd given it a shot in my early twenties, it had quickly become one of my favorite types of sushi)—everything was fresh, and the sweet, salty, tangy flavors exploding on my tongue had me dancing in my chair. Or maybe that was the music.

I liked jazz generally, but the energy of this band was something else. The drums, the guitar, the saxophone, the thump of the bass that was so strong I could feel it vibrating from the floor up through my barstool. As the songs washed over me, I soaked up the vibrant sounds and let loose a series of shoulder shimmies that had Ford laughing and joining in.

We ate until we couldn't stand another bite, getting tipsy on sake all the while. I was sure we'd be heading back to our villa afterward. We'd just spent the entire day pushing our bodies to their limit, and I knew we'd both be sore in the morning. But as Ford signed the check, he began nodding along with the music, looking over toward the stage area where people were cheering and writhing together on the dance floor.

He slapped the pen down, tucked his wallet away, and held out his hand.

"Dance with me, Em," he said with a grin, tugging me out of my seat.

I couldn't resist.

He led me to the dance floor, and I clung to his hand

as we wove our way through the crowd. It was hot and steamy with all the people crushed together, dancing and sweating and singing along with the music. I could barely hear myself think, swept up in the hectic verve of it all, and I loved it. As we hit the floor, I let the music take over. I felt free and alive and unself-conscious, anonymous in a way I never would have if we were home in Chicago.

Dancing, it turned out, was therapeutic. I could finally get all my wild, pent-up energy out. I spun and thrashed and swished my hips, trying to work it out of my system. In the dim light, I could see Ford's eyes glued to me, and it just made me even more wild. In fact, I felt powerful. My husband could watch me all he wanted. Let him eat his heart out.

When the song ended, I was sweating and out of breath. I'd never felt better. I was just about to ask Ford if we could head home when the music slowed to a sultry beat, and he spun me around and circled his arms around my waist. His body was pressed so close to mine that I let out a little moan, and that's when he started grinding against me from behind. Almost without thinking, I pushed back, sliding my hips side to side, my ass brushing his crotch. It was less like dancing and more like giving him a lap dance standing up. He didn't seem to mind.

I could feel his cock—hard and throbbing—through the fabric of his pants, and his hands slid down to my hips, holding me in place as he thrusted against the crack of my ass.

"You're so fucking hot," he whispered into my ear, his husky voice barely audible above the music.

"Mm-hmm," I murmured.

I circled my hips again, slower this time, loving the way

his grip tightened when I did, loving the way he pulled me even closer. And then he started saying the dirtiest things...

"You're gonna come so hard tonight," he growled, "there won't be anything fake about how loud I make you scream."

I shivered with anticipation, turning in his arms so we were face-to-face.

"Tell me more," I mouthed, letting him read my lips.

"I'm going to ruin you for whoever you fuck after me," he went on, his hands sliding up my ribcage, thumbs brushing my tingling nipples through my dress.

I arched against him, wanting so much more.

A riot of emotions tumbled through me. I was upset at the mention of future sex partners, but aroused at the way he was rubbing it in—the fact that he probably already *had* ruined me for anyone else I might ever sleep with. He wasn't just good in bed, he was...intuitive. It was like he always knew exactly what I wanted, what felt good to me, what would get me off.

But two could play at that game, I decided. Because if Ford thought he was going to ruin me for all other lovers, then I wanted to ruin him, too. I would make this night—hell, our whole honeymoon—something he could never forget.

Sliding my hands into his front pockets, I looked up at him as I stroked his length with my fingertips, just enough to tease him. When he let out a helpless groan, I spun around and swirled my ass against his cock, grateful that the dance floor was too packed for anyone to see what we were doing.

His hands were tight on my hips again, holding me so firmly that I would probably have bruises tomorrow, but I didn't care. All of a sudden, I got an idea. A dirty one.

I leaned forward with my hands on my knees, slowly

shimmying my way up until my back was pressed to Ford's chest. What he hadn't noticed was my hand darting under my dress, between my thighs, lightning quick. Giving me just enough time to slide a finger inside my pussy.

Turning in his arms, I smiled naughtily. Then I brought my wet finger to his lips, pushing it into his mouth.

His eyes widened instantly, and then he was sucking my finger, licking it clean, hungry for more. Later, once we got home, I would give it to him.

There was no way we could go back to being friends once this was over. We would have to go our separate ways, and we might not even speak again. But no matter what, I was going to make sure that Ford's memories of me would be searingly erotic.

He wanted to ruin me for others? Two could play at that game.

EMZEE

CHAPTER 5

We were barely through the door of our villa before Ford had flung me up against the wall to attack me with kisses. I moaned into his mouth, the feel of his lips—hot and firm and aggressive—making me ache for him. I'd missed this. His hunger, his touch.

How I ever thought I'd be able to resist him indefinitely was beyond me.

I fumbled with the buttons on his shirt while his hands slid under my dress and up my ass, his short nails gently scraping my skin and giving me goosebumps. I felt the cool brush of air against my thong as he shoved his thigh between my legs, pinning me to the wall. Somehow, amidst all the frantic groping, I managed to tug his shirt over his shoulders and down his arms.

We were both still damp with sweat from the hot dance floor, and each other.

"Come on," Ford said, pressing a kiss against the hollow of my throat. "Let's get you cleaned up." It would be my second shower of the day. Not that I was complaining.

The villa's master bathroom was approximately the size of my first studio apartment. There was a huge glass-walled shower with multiple showerheads, all going in different directions. It was luxurious and tasteful, with wall-to-wall marble and gleaming brass fixtures.

Ford made short work of the rest of my dress, pulling it over my head and leaving me in nothing but my scrap of a thong. I wasn't wearing a bra, and he let out a groan of appreciation when my breasts were bared to him. Looping his finger into the waistband of my underwear, he gave a sharp tug and the delicate fabric ripped, causing the whole thing to come off in his hand.

I gasped with surprise and pleasure. "What have you done?" I said with a teasing grin.

"I regret nothing. You should never wear panties," Ford said.

He was kissing me again before I could reply, pulling off his shoes and pants until he was naked too. I could feel his cock—huge and hard and hot—jutting against me. Reaching down, I gripped it in my hand and gave him a long stroke. Once upon a time, I would have never been so bold, but the day had given me a new sense of power and confidence. First with the windsurfing and then with the dancing. It felt like I had a new connection to my body and I wanted to take advantage of it.

Ford seemed more than eager to let me do what I wanted, but after a few more strokes of my hand, he was leading me toward the shower and twisting the taps so hot water came out.

"Get in," he said. I obeyed.

The water was the perfect temperature, sluicing down on us to wash away the sweat from the club, glistening deliciously over the hard planes of Ford's body.

46

"Come here," he said. So commanding.

He grabbed the soap and started working up a lather, never taking his eyes off me.

"I think there's a very dirty girl in here that needs to get clean," he said.

"Not too clean," I purred.

Without a word he pulled me closer, trailing handfuls of soapy, bubbling foam from my shoulders to my wrists. The parts of my body that ached most for him—my breasts, between my thighs—went untouched as he lathered up my back, down my legs, even my feet. God, this man was good with his hands. Getting a massage from Ford Malone was like a little slice of heaven.

Finally, finally, he began to massage my breasts, making big circles with his firm but slick hands. I leaned my head back against the wall, letting out a full-throated moan as the sensations overwhelmed me. The warmth of his hands, the slide of the water, the slip of the soap, it all felt incredible. My nipples were tingling, emerging from the bubbles only to be stroked by Ford's talented hands. He gave my nipples a firm, punishing twist that I loved, and then began moving downward.

Eager to be touched, I spread my legs wide as he knelt between them.

Looking up at me, he narrowed his eyes. "Tell me what you want."

This game again.

"You," I said, trying to pull his hand between my legs, and failing.

"Say it. Say the words," he goaded.

"I want you to finger me," I said, my cheeks going even hotter than they already were.

"Mmm, that's good," Ford said approvingly. "You want

to feel my fingers in your sweet little pussy? My hot tongue, lapping you up?"

My knees buckled at his dirty talk, but I placed my palms on the wall behind me to keep me upright.

"Fuck yes," I said, swallowing thickly. I was so ready. So needy. "Do it. Please."

But Ford didn't touch me yet.

"Tell me *exactly* what you want," he said, grinning wickedly. "Tell me and I'll do it."

This wasn't what I had planned at all. I wanted to seduce him, to ruin him. But I couldn't resist what I knew he could give me. Not when I knew how good he was at...everything.

"I want your mouth on my pussy," I said. "I want you to eat me out until I come."

"Good girl," Ford said, and then he lowered his head to taste me.

I cried out as his tongue speared me deep. There was no gentleness now, no teasing. He was going hard and fast, using his tongue to fuck me against the shower wall, and I loved it. I wanted more. I widened my stance and he used his fingers to spread my lips, his tongue circling my clit before diving back inside of me.

"Yes," I panted. "Yes, fuck yes."

I was moaning now, my hips rolling toward him, unable to control myself. My body was his to command, to control, to pleasure. And just like always, he knew exactly what I wanted.

He stretched me even wider with his fingers and then one was pumping inside of me, then two, his hand fucking me while his tongue lapped at my clit. The water was spilling hot and fast around us, but I barely noticed, I was so caught up in what Ford was doing to me.

Then, without warning, my orgasm slammed into me. I let out a deep, helpless moan, the sound echoing off the walls, holding on to Ford's broad shoulders as I rode out the waves.

Once I'd caught my breath, I started to lower myself to my knees, but Ford stopped me. He shut off the water and then spun me around and pushed me toward the glass door. I could feel his cock, hard and ready against my ass. We grabbed our towels, but had barely started to dry off before Ford was bending me over the vanity.

I gripped the marble countertop, my body humming with anticipation as he came up behind me. He started tracing my entrance with the tip of his cock and I pushed my ass back to help guide him inside, but once again he stopped me, taking full control.

"You want this big fucking cock?" he asked, smacking it against my ass.

"Yes," I moaned, a rush of adrenaline coursing through me. God yes I did.

"What do you want?" he asked. "Say the words."

"I want your cock," I begged, my voice cracking. "I want your big fucking cock."

His voice was hot in my ear as he grabbed me by the hair and jerked my head back, bringing me to the sweet intersection of pleasure and pain. "You want me to fuck you like this? From behind? While you watch in the mirror?"

"Yes," I moaned. "I want to watch. I want to watch you fuck me."

With a low groan, he thrusted hard inside me, both of us moaning at the deep connection. He released my hair so I could fulfill my pledge to watch our reflection, his hands sliding down to grip my hips tightly. For a moment we just stayed there like that, our eyes locked in the mirror, Ford's cock buried in me, my hands gripping the counter, my breasts swaying heavily, my pussy throbbing.

"Do it," I whispered. "Fuck me."

Then he began to move.

He slowly pulled out, giving my ass a hard, stinging slap. Then, with a growl, he slammed back inside, taking my breath away. Somehow, he was able to fill me up even more. His thrusts were fast, frantic, pushing me against the edge of the vanity. It felt animalistic and out of control and absolutely hot.

"Look at those tits bounce," Ford said, pounding rhythmically. "You like that?"

"I love it," I groaned.

"God, you're fucking perfect," he gasped, fucking me even faster and harder, and I realized that my dirty talk was just as intoxicating to him as his wicked words were to me. I saw my chance to push him over the edge, so I did it. I took control, arching my back so he could pump even deeper, rocking my hips in time to meet every thrust of his cock.

I wanted to make sure he never forgot this night. I started moaning louder, letting loose everything I felt inside, giving voice to all the pleasure building up. I let it all out, glad we had an entire house to ourselves to fill with the sounds of our fucking. I wanted him to know what he was doing to me, wanted him to feel it from his head to his toes to his fucking balls.

"Fuck me, Ford," I moaned. "Fuck my tight little pussy. Make me come on your cock."

"Jesus, Em," he groaned, breathing so fast and heavy that I was sure he had worked up a sweat all over again.

"Yes, Ford, yes," I yelled, pitching my voice high like a porn star. I loved what I was doing to him, making him lose himself, his eyes closed as he let out a breathless stream of curses.

It was clear that the sex we'd had last night—decent, but so "bare minimum" as to be forgettable—wasn't worth it. Especially when I was reminded of what I was missing. I wouldn't resort to it again. Not a chance.

This was what I wanted. Hot, dirty, passionate sex. No inhibitions, no shame. The kind of sex that would be seared into Ford's memory and my own.

The sound of sex filled the bathroom, the chorus of our grunts and moans along with Ford's hips hitting the back of my legs with solid, hot slaps. I could feel every inch of him inside of me, could feel another climax building with every thrust.

Still gripping my hip with one hand, Ford brought the other one down to my clit. As he speared into me from behind, he squeezed my clit, the dual sensation of his cock and his hand pushing me over the edge.

"I'm coming," I said, my gaze still glued to our reflection. "Watch me come, Ford."

But it was Ford who came first, gasping as he spilled into me, our eyes locked in the mirror. He was still coming when my own orgasm hit, my body clenching tight around his cock as I cried out my pleasure. When I finally stopped shaking, I realized that he was still hard and buried deep inside me. I'd expected him to pull out and collapse in a heap, but instead, he withdrew from my body and pulled me into the bedroom.

"How are you still hard?" I asked, trying to catch my breath.

"Magic," he said with a laugh. "You want to go again?"

"Oh my God. Seriously?" My knees were weak, but

when he pushed me down on the bed, I knew I wanted another round. "I want to be on top."

His eyebrows rose with surprise, but his eyes went even darker with desire.

"Whatever my wife wants," he said.

I tried to ignore the thrill I got from being referred to as his wife, and instead gave him a push so that he fell back onto the bed. I watched his face as I climbed onto him, his gaze going from my face to my breasts and then lower. He licked his lips, and I wanted to do the same. Seeing Ford stretched out on the bed in all his naked glory made me hot. It seemed impossible that I would still want more after the two explosive orgasms he'd already given me, but as I guided him back inside me, I realized that when it came to Ford Malone, I might be insatiable.

The feeling seemed mutual.

I straddled Ford, his cock sliding into me deliciously, his hands coming up to rest on my hips. I half expected him to take charge again, but he let me set the pace. I spread my legs wide, my knees on either side of his hips. Then I started rocking. His eyes were dark with lust, and I knew I was giving him a perfect view of his favorite parts of my body.

"Mmm," I moaned, taking my sweet time to slowly pick up speed.

I fucked him hard but slow, reminding him wordlessly that I had control in this—even though it often felt like I didn't have control over anything else in my life. As I sank lower onto him, I realized I wanted to make him come. Wanted him to shatter into a million pieces.

"Ford," I said breathily. "You feel so good."

Arching my back, I thrust my breasts forward and tilted my head back. I wanted Ford to watch my tits bounce as I fucked him.

I began to move faster and faster. As I did, I used my inner muscles to squeeze Ford tightly. He let out a choked moan, his hands sliding up to cup my breasts, his fingers pinching my nipples. I knew he wanted me to come first, but I wasn't going to allow that. He needed to know that right now, I was the one in charge.

And I was going to give him an orgasm he'd never forget.

"Em," he choked out. I could tell that he was getting close, but didn't want to let go.

Too bad I wasn't giving him a choice.

I leaned into his hands, his fingers still squeezing my nipples as I began to raise and lower myself on his cock, taking him deeper each time. I could feel my own orgasm racing toward me and my fingers slipped down to my wet, slippery clit.

"You're so deep," I moaned. "So deep in my pussy."

His breaths were getting more shallow and I knew he was doing everything he could to hold back.

"I want to feel you come," I purred, egging him on. "I want you to come so hard."

I was moving faster and faster, rubbing my clit while I squeezed my inner muscles around Ford's cock, all the friction and heat between us reaching the point of no return.

"Fuck!" he gasped, losing all control, grabbing my hips and pulling me down on his cock as he thrust up inside me in hot, shuddering spurts. "Emzee," he was moaning, over and over.

It was all I needed to send me over the edge. My orgasm began to crest, and I shut my eyes and whispered Ford's name, bracing myself against his shoulders as the pleasure spread through me in rippling waves, my whole body shaking with the intensity of it. It felt endless.

Afterward I lay there, head against Ford's chest. As I listened to his pounding heartbeat, I knew without a doubt that he would never, ever forget this night.

EMZEE

CHAPTER 6

I was home in Chicago again, and thank God.

The romantic environment of St. Barts—and the fact that Ford and I had fucked on nearly every surface in the villa—had made it impossible to keep my feelings at bay for the rest of our trip. But despite the fantasy, I'd known we couldn't stay in our little bubble forever. Because no matter how hot the sex had been, no matter how romantic the honeymoon, none of that changed the reality of our situation.

In less than a year, I'd have to divorce Ford and walk away for good.

Which meant that I had to go back to protecting my heart.

Unfortunately, my head was still swimming with indelible memories of the two of us in paradise. We'd picnicked on the beach every day, marveling at the weather and the free-roaming iguanas. Most afternoons we windsurfed, swam, or went snorkeling, genuinely enjoying each other's company all the while. And Ford had made my foodie dreams come true by taking me to the island's best restaurants for dinner each night. Our concierge Phillipe had proven to be an invaluable resource for recommendations of both Michelin-worthy places offering leisurely, lavish, multi-course meals as well as the lesser known beachside spots where you could get insanely good ceviche, spicy Creole food, fresh mahi-mahi en brochette, and rum punch.

Sigh.

Now that we were back, things would return to normal. We'd settle into a routine. I had my job and Ford had his, so our days would be busy and spent mostly apart. The only time we'd really see each other would be at night, and though I figured neither of us would be avoiding sex, at least there wouldn't be much time for romancing in between. Which I told myself was a good thing. I had to keep my head on straight.

If the next year of our marriage was basically just a lot of hot sex without too much emotion, maybe I could survive this whole thing with most of my heart intact.

However, before we could begin our new life, there was one big task that we needed to undertake.

We had to officially move in together.

Obviously, Ford's apartment made more sense for us, being bigger and newer and more practical compared to my loft's mostly open floor plan and complete lack of spare rooms. But for the past few months we'd held off, telling anyone who asked that I was a little old-fashioned about cohabitating and wanted to wait until after we tied the knot to move in. Since Claudia had lived with him before, it wasn't an excuse Ford could have used, but everyone seemed to accept that he'd agreed in order to please me.

I was grateful for the distraction that the move gave me. Even though I was keeping my loft as a studio space for work (which was a legitimate need), Munchkin and I still had to make ourselves at home at Ford's to really sell the charade of our marriage. But knowing I'd be moving right back in eleven months hence, I left most of my furniture at the loft. All I really needed were my clothes, toiletries, and a few other sundry items.

And then moving day was upon us. There was no turning back.

Following the movers into Ford's apartment, I couldn't help frowning. I'd been over plenty of times, so the uber masculine look of the place—clashing hideously with Claudia's ultra-girly touches—was no surprise to me. And given the temporary nature of the move, I knew I shouldn't voice my opinions about the furnishings and design. It wasn't my permanent home, after all, so there was no point in making a big deal about the décor.

But I couldn't help myself.

I'd always been loud and clear about my feelings regarding Ford's bachelor pad. Both before and after Claudia's hideous "styling" of the place, which had given me the overall impression that a Barbie Dreamhouse and a Ralph Lauren catalog had conspired to simultaneously explode all over Ford's leather-and-brushed steel wet dream. It was a nightmare.

My very un-secret opinion of the place was partly why we always hung out at my loft.

As I looked around, it was obvious that Claudia's touch was still all over the place. From the cloying, heavy scent of her designer candles on the entryway table, to the metallic gold throw pillows on the armchair, to the flowery curtains and huge framed print in the bathroom that said, in a bright pink script font, "Hello, gorgeous!"

It had to go.

I had just finished unpacking my clothes into the

dresser and walk-in closet Ford had provided for my exclusive use when I heard the front door open. Munchkin was off like a shot, panting as he scrambled to greet Ford. I was excited to see my new husband, too...because I was more than ready to discuss what would need to change if I was going to live here.

"Em?" Ford called out from down the hall.

"I'm in your room!" I called back.

"*Our* room," he corrected, stepping through the doorway in his crisp work suit with my slobbery dog in his arms. "You all unpacked?"

God, could that man make me melt in an instant. That suit, that jawline, the obvious affection for my furbaby...the way he freaking smelled.

"Almost," I said, recovering my senses. "Just a few more boxes."

"Great," he said, setting down Munchkin. "What do you want to do for dinner?"

"Actually, I wanted to talk to you about decorating," I said.

Ford looked around, clearly puzzled.

"Decorating what?" he asked. "The place is already decorated."

"By you," I said. "And Claudia."

He looked at me blankly. "Are you serious? Claudia's long gone. You know that."

"That's not the point," I said. "Besides, no girl ever moved into a new place without adding her touch. It would be totally obvious that this was an act if someone came over and saw that nothing had changed since your ex-girlfriend left."

Ford rolled his eyes. "Fine. What were you thinking?"

I had a whole list. We started in the living room.

"New paint in here," I said, gesturing to the dark walls. "Don't get me wrong, I obviously love black, but I prefer lighter colored walls. It helps a space feel more airy and open."

"It's called a man *cave* for a reason," Ford shot back. "Besides, it's not black. It's navy. Makes it cozy in here."

"A different shade of blue then, maybe cobalt?" I saw him visibly recoil. "Fine, what about slate blue? That's cozy."

"Navy matches the sofa," he pointed out. "It's a good contrast with the cognac leather."

Was he planning to counter my every suggestion? "New sofa then," I snapped.

Ford shook his head.

"Nu-uh," he said. "I love this thing. It's comfortable as hell and I've had it since college, so it's perfectly molded to my body. The couch stays."

Record scratch.

"You're telling me you've had this *since college?*" I asked.

"Yep," Ford said, looking proud. "Just look at the patina that's built up over the years. You can't buy that."

I was horrified. Now all I'd be able think of when I looked at the couch was how many girls a frisky, younger Ford had fooled around with on that leather. Patina my ass. The last thing I wanted to do was sit on a surface where Ford had messed around with a bunch of sorority girls. Not to mention whatever he'd done on it with Claudia.

"We have to change something," I said, feeling like this was going nowhere.

"No one hangs out in the living room anyway," Ford said. "The den and the bedroom are where we'll be spending most of our time."

I hated the den. Mainly because of one thing.

"If you expect me to hang out in the den, you'll need to get rid of the painting," I said, crossing my arms. "That thing is god-awful."

It was a huge oil on canvas done in an abstract style, depicting a naked woman kneeling in front of a fully clothed man. I could tell that it was vintage, and it had a nice gold frame, but I hated it. Not only did it seem kind of creepy and voyeuristic—not in a good way—but it practically took up the entire wall. There was no escaping it.

"That painting is art!" Ford said. "It's an original Le Comte, and it cost me a fortune. It stays."

He plopped down on the couch with his arms behind his head and I could tell there was no negotiating. For every suggestion I made, for every single room in the house, Ford had some dumb reason why we couldn't change anything. By the time the conversation was over, I'd gotten him to throw out the cutesy print hanging in the bathroom and agree to let me pick out a new bath mat and shower curtain, but that was it. I felt exhausted and demoralized.

I retreated into the bedroom to finish unpacking, but for a moment I just stared at the boxes. Should I even bother? Would Ford actually let me put my own books and photos on his shelves in the living room, or would he have some excuse for why they couldn't go there?

Sinking onto the edge of the bed, I pulled Munchkin onto my lap and rested my chin on the top of his blocky little head. I was starting to realize that there was no hope for me and Ford at all. Even if his parents hadn't given our marriage a deadline, it was obvious that Ford never had any intention of moving forward with me. He wasn't even close to being ready.

He just wanted everything to stay the same.

That was the whole reason he had decided to embark on this charade with me in the first place—because he knew that with me, he wouldn't have to make any changes in his life. He knew I would go along with whatever he wanted, no matter what. It was the reason he'd always wanted our friendship to stay the same.

I hated that I was essentially proving him right.

Ford was the kind of guy who was completely comfortable with what he had, and just wanted to maintain status quo. He wanted his couch to stay the same, the color of his walls, the painting in his den. Everything exactly the same, including our dynamic. And he wanted a wife who would let him live his life exactly the way he always had. The way *he* wanted it.

It was going to be a long year.

CHAPTER 7

Even though it felt pointless, I unpacked my books anyway. It was like having old friends around, displaying my favorite photography hardcovers depicting the work of Man Ray or detailing the world's ancient ruins or Polaroids of colorful NYC nightlife in the 1970s, or—because playful images were just as valuable as serious ones—dogs swimming underwater. I had just finished arranging them on my dresser and nightstand, the moving boxes already broken down and stacked in the corner, when Ford came into the bedroom.

"My parents are coming to dinner," he said.

"What?" I stared at him. "When? Tonight?"

"Seven-thirty."

That was barely two hours away. There was so much to do. *Shit.*

I immediately leapt up and ran to the kitchen. A quick inspection of the fridge and bare cupboards confirmed my worst nightmare. We had nothing.

"I could have used a little warning," I told Ford, scrambling for my keys and shoes.

He shrugged. "They didn't ask," he said. "They just called and said they were coming over. They do that sometimes. Claudia never minded."

Ah. Of course the senior Malones had just gone ahead and invited themselves to dinner. Because our marriage was apparently under their purview, as was our apartment. Even in what was now my own "home," it was clear I had absolutely no control over anything.

Clenching my jaw, I left the apartment to go shopping. Half to keep myself from throttling Ford and half because I needed to prepare for the arrival of my in-laws.

If I couldn't change the way the apartment was decorated and I couldn't control when Ford's parents came over for dinner, I could at least control what we ate and how I served it.

On my drive over to the mall, I used the hands-free in my car to call in a delivery order at a local Caribbean restaurant for fresh seafood, a few different salads, and grilled veggies. I missed St. Barts, and wanted to bring the taste of the Caribbean back. Not being the best cook, I figured that rushing around in an attempt to throw something together for my in-laws would be ill advised. And I really didn't want our apartment to smell like fish when they arrived.

Relieved that a delicious dinner would soon be on the way, I dashed into Williams Sonoma and switched my focus to shopping for items that would create an unforgettable table setting to impress the Malones—what I'd seen referred to in lifestyle magazines as a "tablescape." With the cuisine I'd chosen, I thought it would be fun to go with a beachy theme to recreate some of the magic of the honeymoon. I was actually kind of excited.

Back at Ford's, loaded down with shopping bags, I let the inspiration take me. I put a fishing net on the table instead of a cloth, circled the pillar candles in the center with assorted seashells, and then set out some new ocean-blue plates, terra-cotta colored napkins, and wooden utensils. With a flash of genius, I realized I could tie little bows around the napkins with pieces of twine, hinting at nautical rope.

The whole color scheme reminded me so much of St. Barts, I couldn't help wishing Ford and I were still there.

Sure, things had been getting more complicated emotionally the longer we'd stayed. But it had also been nice to get away from all the stress (and secrets) his family had fomented in our lives. When it was just me and Ford, all we had to worry about was whether or not we wanted to go out windsurfing or stay in and fuck each other's brains out all over our villa.

Feeling a distracting tug in my lower belly, I shook the sexy memories away and stepped back to admire my handiwork. The table looked even better than I had expected. Seconds later the doorbell rang. My adrenaline surged.

It was our food delivery, not the Malones. Thank God. I was relieved to find the order was not only on time, but also correct and smelling amazing. Ford had just finished helping me plate everything in the kitchen and pick out a bottle of wine when we heard a knock.

"That's them," he said, walking past me to get the door. Munchkin followed after him, tail wagging like crazy.

Even though I was still annoyed at Ford for springing his parents on me like this, I couldn't help admiring how sexy he was. He'd changed into a black shirt, unbuttoned at the neck, and a pair of jeans that fit him perfectly. I confess my knees went a little weak when he glanced back to give me a grin before opening the door.

My happiness faded the moment his parents walked in.

Mrs. Malone immediately put a hand to her chest, pressing her back to the wall. "Ford, dear, you know I can't stand dogs!" she scolded as Munchkin sniffed politely at Mr. Malone's outstretched hand.

"Sorry about that—I'll put him in his kennel," I said, rushing to scoop up my apparently offensive, eighteen-pound dog. "Be right back."

When I returned, they were chatting warmly with Ford in the living room. Seeing me, the Malones' smiles grew visibly tighter.

Neither of them actually greeted me.

"Welcome!" I said as brightly as possible. "Please, won't you come sit down?"

"We're *so* glad to have you back," Mrs. Malone said, ignoring me as she looked back at Ford. "You were gone for much too long."

"We were on our honeymoon," Ford reminded her as he ushered his parents toward the dining room. "I think we were entitled to some vacation time after the wedding."

Ford's mother shrugged and then came to a dead halt when she saw the table.

I held my breath, swelling with pride, knowing that it looked incredible.

"It's a tablescape," I explained grandly. "I wanted to bring a little bit of St. Barts home to Chicago."

"It looks...nice," offered Mr. Malone, pulling out a chair for his wife.

"Hmm," Mrs. Malone said, sitting down gingerly. "A little ostentatious, truth be told."

I wilted.

"And this..." She touched the edge of the fishing net we were using as a tablecloth. "Did this come out of the garbage?"

"*Mother*," Ford warned.

"Of course not," I said. "It's brand new."

She shrugged.

"Well, I'm starving," Ford's father said, glancing around.

"I'll go ahead and get everyone served so we can eat," I said, inching toward the kitchen.

"Must we?" I heard Ford's mother ask as I left the room.

"Mother," Ford said again, sharper this time. "Be nice."

"You know I'm just teasing," she responded.

But she wasn't. And when dinner came out, it only got worse.

"What is this?" she asked, wrinkling her nose at the food I'd put down in front of her.

"Oxtail stew, conch fritters, and a whole snapper," I told her.

Her scowl deepened. "This fish is frowning at me. And Ford, you know spicy food doesn't agree with your father's digestion. Did you make this, Mara?"

I honestly didn't know what would be worse—if I *had* made it, or if I admitted the truth.

"It's actually from Garifuna Flava," I said. "This really wonderful Caribbean restaurant here in Chicago."

"I see," she sniffed. "Keeping with the whole honeymoon theme. How quaint."

I sat down, in full-blown panic mode. This was just the start of our meal. I prayed it wouldn't get worse.

It did.

My efforts to put together a nice meal were all for naught, because apparently nothing I'd done was right. Not only were the decorations tacky, not only was the food too spicy and not "elevated" enough for their refined palates, but Ford's mother made it a point to continually harp on all the ways that Claudia had done things better.

"I remember the last time we had dinner with the two of you," she mused, picking at her salad. It was the only thing on her plate that she'd touched.

Of course, she wasn't talking about me, but about Ford and Claudia.

"We had the most perfect filet mignon and asparagus souffle served on china plates," she said. "And a private chef to make it all! Truly one of the best meals I've ever had."

She poked at her fish a couple of times, didn't bother to try any of it, and eventually pushed the plate away. There was a bottle of wine at the center of the table, and though I'd filled everyone's glasses when we first sat down, Ford's mother's was now empty and she looked at me with expectant eyes, clearing her throat. The bottle, of course, was closer to her.

"Would you like some more wine?" I asked.

"I would," she said, turning to her husband. "Do you remember how Claudia always made sure our glasses were full? She would never have to ask."

Ford's father was busy eating—apparently the spices tasted just fine to him, despite his wife's criticism. Meanwhile, Ford said nothing.

I poured the wine, but with my hands shaking, some of it spilled on the table.

Ford's mother looked at me as if I'd spilled it directly on her.

"Well, I suppose it doesn't matter," she said, narrowing her eyes at her glass. "This wine isn't a very good vintage, after all. Claudia always made sure to have my favorite Pinot whenever we came over."

I was pretty sure that if I heard Claudia's name again, I would throw something. The message was clear: I wasn't good enough for Ford, and I never would be.

"Would anyone like dessert?" I asked. "It's sorbet. Coconut." The scoops were all ready to go in the freezer, in pretty blue glass bowls, topped with a sprig of mint.

"Sounds great," Ford said. "I'll help you clear the dishes."

I wished he would defend me—and the meal—to his parents, but as usual, his mom was being a total steamroller. It seemed like Ford was just trying to get through the meal in one piece, as was I. But when I finally put dessert down, Mrs. Malone pushed the bowls aside.

"And now the real reason for this visit. We need to speak with you two about something very important," Ford's mother said.

His father was looking all around the room—anywhere but at me or Ford. Whatever this was about, I doubted he would say anything. Mrs. Malone was steering the ship. Per usual.

I braced myself, not knowing what to expect, but still expecting the worst.

"I know that you're newlyweds," Ford's mother said. "And that you're...having fun."

Ford gagged. "Mother," he said. "We don't need to discuss this."

"Oh, please." Ford's mother waved her hand. "All I'm saying is that you two need to be careful. It's far too soon for children. You're both so young."

Ah. Right. So even though I'd agreed to divorce Ford within the year, she wasn't content with my promise. She wanted to make sure there wouldn't be any new Malone offspring that would keep Ford tied to me—legally, financially, emotionally, or otherwise—in the future.

"We're not even thinking about it," Ford said. "Though honestly, this isn't your business. It's ours."

"Ford's right," I agreed, noticing that Mr. Malone had somehow managed to make his entire bowl of sorbet disappear while the rest of us had been distracted.

I discreetly slid my bowl over to him, having thoroughly lost my appetite.

"You should both be focusing on your careers at this stage of your lives," Ford's mother went on. "And I'm certain Mara wouldn't want to sacrifice her photography— not while she's already struggling to make a name for herself in such a competitive field. Which, honestly..."

It wouldn't be Mother Malone if she couldn't find a way to compliment and insult me at the same time. With every word, every sentence, I felt smaller and smaller.

It was clear that this lecture wasn't actually directed at Ford. It was Mrs. Malone's way of not-so-subtly reminding me of our agreement, and the fact that I was expendable. That she'd do everything in her power to make sure that after the year was up, I'd be gone as planned. The threat of not paying off the Bratva was underneath all of it, of course, right under the surface.

The worst part was listening to Ford bend over backwards to agree with everything his mom was saying, which gave me the sinking feeling—yet again—that there really was no hope for us. It was the same feeling I'd had since this afternoon, when Ford refused to change anything in the apartment. And that was when it dawned on me.

Ford didn't want to change the apartment *because* Claudia had lived here with him. I could see it all so clearly now. He *liked* the way Claudia had done things. Just like his parents did. Because Claudia wasn't just perfect—she was perfect for him.

Ford must still be in love with her.

And me? I was just a distraction he was having fun

banging. Maybe even part of a larger plot Ford had master-minded in order to make Claudia jealous—jealous enough to grovel and beg and bend to his every wish when she inevitably came back around.

And there wasn't anything I could do about it. All I could do was perform the role I had agreed to play for the rest of the year, to the best of my ability. So that when this was all over, I'd never have to deal with the Malone family again.

Exactly the way they wanted.

EMZEE

CHAPTER 8

By the time the Malones finally said their goodbyes and the leftover food and dirty dishes were all squared away, I wanted nothing more than to take a long, hot, soul-cleansing shower and go directly to bed.

Ideally alone.

I hated that I couldn't go back to the sanctuary of my own apartment. I hated that I was trapped, living in what felt like a memorial to Ford's ex-girlfriend.

Before I could make my retreat, though, Ford followed me into the bedroom, an unreadable expression on his face.

"I know what you're thinking," he said.

"Oh really?" I snarked. "Do tell."

I didn't even try to hide my irritation. Who could blame me? He was the reason I'd gotten into this whole wedding mess in the first place. Specifically because he hadn't wanted his parents pushing him with Claudia. And now this?

"You think I'm still in love with Claudia," he said.

"Why would I think that?" I asked, all sarcasm. "Because you didn't stop your parents from talking about her all night? Or—oh—maybe because you can't bear to part with anything she touched in this apartment?"

"That's not what—" Ford started.

"It's no big deal," I cut him off, "any girl would be flattered. In fact, what kind of wife *wouldn't* be thrilled to live in an apartment where she's constantly reminded of her husband's ex? I love it."

"This is how you want to be?" he said. "Come on, then. Let me give you the proper tour."

Grabbing me by the arm, he pulled me out of the room and down the hall. In the living room, both of us huffing, I was steered over to the bookcase.

"This vase?" Ford spat, pointing to a beautiful, reddish brown piece of pottery with an intricate pattern carved into it. "We got that in Sri Lanka. We spent the day at Polonnaruwa and a group of women were selling things outside the entrance. She said she wanted something to remember the day by, since I first told her I loved her in front of the Parakrama Samudra."

My stomach was in knots so tight that I felt sick, but I didn't walk away. Instead, I let him turn me around and push me to the glass-fronted cabinet in the dining room.

Ford flung open the doors, revealing shelves of neatly stacked porcelain dishes with a delicate red pattern visible at the edges.

"That china my mom was talking about? I still have it, right here in the sideboard. Claudia chose the pattern because my grandmother used to have the same one and she wanted to build on tradition together."

My eyes were stinging, but I refused to let my tears spill over. Ford was hurting me on purpose, and I didn't want to give him the satisfaction of seeing me crack.

Next up was the den, where I had to look at the

obscenely huge, vaguely erotic painting that I hated so much.

"This painting?" Ford growled. "The one you hate? It's by an artist Claudia and I once met at a gallery opening that neither of us wanted to be at. We'd fought all day beforehand and the first time we'd spoken in four hours was to agree that we both loved it. It became a symbol of communication for us."

As we went from room to room, Ford telling me the stories of all his precious fucking belongings, the tension built between us. Ford's eyes seemed to burn into mine and the way he was looking at me, I couldn't tell if he wanted to throttle me or rip my clothes off. I honestly couldn't decide which one I wanted either.

Finally, we made it into his office. Both of us stared at the antique desk that stood against the wall.

"This desk?" Ford slapped his hand on it.

The sound made me jump, but I wasn't scared. I was turned on. The anger I felt had begun to morph into lust and I could tell by the way Ford's eyes kept raking up and down my body that he was feeling the same way.

"Tell me," I said.

"You want to know about this desk?" he asked, advancing on me.

I nodded and he grabbed me by the hips to shove me toward it, pressing my ass up against the edge. With one simple lift, Ford could have me sitting on top of it.

"We bought it in Paris," Ford said, his face close to mine, his voice low in my ear.

His fingers tightened against my hips and I pressed against him. He was hard. I was wet. I wanted him, and he wanted me.

"How nice for you two," I said, glaring.

"At a famous flea market," he continued. As he did, he began unbuttoning my shirt. "The seller swore that Hemingway had once written on it."

My shirt was hanging open now, exposing my lace bra. Ford reached out and gave the front clasp a little flick, and my breasts spilled out.

Breathing hard, he reached out and cupped them, his thumbs dragging over my nipples more roughly than they ever had before. I arched into his touch. I wanted more.

"Tell me," I ordered.

I spread my legs and his hands dropped to unbutton my pants and yank them off, my thong going with them in one fast, rough movement. In half a second, I was naked and Ford was hoisting me onto the desk. He was grinding against me, cock straining behind the zipper of his jeans. Groaning, I opened my legs wider, wrapping my legs around him.

"Tell me," I repeated, my voice throaty.

"You want me to tell you that we didn't believe for a second that Hemingway had written on it?" he asked, slapping one hand on the desk behind me, the other undoing his jeans, his hard cock springing free.

"Yes," I said, my mouth watering at the sight.

"But since we'd been drinking Death in the Afternoons all day, the whole thing felt fated, so we spent an exorbitant amount of money on it?"

"Yes," I moaned as he traced the slit of my wet pussy with his tip.

I was so hungry for him, I leaned back on my hands, opening my legs even wider. He must have liked what he saw.

"Fuck, Em," he said, gripping his cock as he panted.

"Fuck me," I agreed, tilting my hips to guide him.

"*Yes*," he said, and with a smooth, fast thrust, he was inside.

I gasped as he filled me up, so big and so deep. Gripping the edge of the desk, I bit my lip as he began fucking me, whispering low in my ear as he picked up his pace.

"You think the shit in my apartment is important to me because I'm still into her?" he asked, punctuating his words with slow, hard thrusts.

"Yes," I moaned, throwing my head back, his mouth coming down to suck my throat. I felt near to tears again, overwhelmed with emotion and all the sensations that went along with having hot, angry sex with my husband.

"Then what do you think it means that I'm fucking my wife on a desk that I bought with her?"

That was the problem. I didn't know what it meant. Was it some kind of filthy erotic game for him? Tearing me down just to fuck me afterward in all my humiliation and rage?

I was simultaneously so hot and angry and turned on that I couldn't think straight. All I could focus on was Ford's cock, pumping in and out as he rode me hard on top of the desk he'd bought with Claudia in Paris.

"Ford," I cried out.

"That's right," he said, driving himself even deeper. "I'm your husband. I'm your fucking husband and I'm fucking your tight, sweet little pussy on this desk."

It creaked beneath us, each thrust knocking it against the wall.

I never thought I'd be into hate sex, but I loved how it made me feel. How heightened it all was. How powerful I felt, that I could drive Ford to this point, where he was practically out of control with desire for me. Because that's how I felt with him. Out of control.

He gripped my hips and fucked me even harder, watching my breasts bounce with every thrust.

I was completely naked and he was still fully dressed. He ducked his head to take my nipple in his mouth and I moaned as he nipped me with his teeth. That combination of pleasure and pain was everything I wanted and only Ford knew how to give it to me. I knew I'd never ever find a man that could satisfy me the way that he did.

I still didn't know what he was trying to do, what he thought he was accomplishing with all of this. Was it just a hot love triangle in his mind? Making me jealous while remembering what it had been like with Claudia, secretly comparing me to her while he fucked me?

Or was he trying to show me how trivial all these objects were to him? Was he tainting his memories of her on purpose?

I didn't have any answers. All I had was the sweet ache between my legs, the delicious feel of Ford's perfect cock, his breath against my ear, bringing me closer and closer to climaxing. I wrapped my legs higher around his waist, leaning back, letting him go even deeper.

"More," I murmured. "Give me more."

He let out a grunt and I could sense that he was close. Hot little sparks were firing off inside my pussy, and I knew when I came—and soon—it would be explosive. The pleasure was barreling toward me, building in my lower belly, making my toes curl as my legs tightened around Ford.

As if he could sense I was about to come, he started fucking me faster. My head was banging against the wall now, but I didn't care.

I didn't care that this was the desk he'd bought with Claudia. I didn't even care if he had done exactly the same thing with her on it that he was doing with me. Right now, all I cared about was chasing my release. I needed it.

"Come for me, Emzee. I want to feel that pussy clench around my cock," Ford said.

It was enough to push me over the edge.

I gasped, coming hard and fast around his cock, doing exactly as he requested. As my body contracted in tight bursts, he let out a hoarse cry and spilled his seed into me, the two of us moaning as we slumped back onto the desk.

As we caught our breath, I realized that even though Ford might never give me any solid answers about Claudia, he'd still given me a fantastic orgasm.

Considering the terms of our relationship, that would have to be enough.

FORD

CHAPTER 9

Even though I'd lived with Claudia, and was used to sharing space with a woman, everything about cohabitating with Emzee felt different. *Everything.*

Take this morning, even, when I'd rolled over in bed to find that Em and I had slept in past 10 o'clock. Claudia never would have allowed that, even on a Saturday like today. She firmly agreed with the science that said sleeping in on the weekend threw off one's circadian rhythms, setting one up for a sluggish Monday at the office.

I hadn't slept so soundly in years.

It was all so new and weird.

After the fight last night, and the incredible sex Emzee and I'd had on that stupid desk in my office, I didn't quite know where my wife and I stood. Our argument hadn't actually been resolved, and it wasn't the kind of thing that was going to figure itself out. As soon as she was up, we'd have to talk about it.

Right now, though, she was fast asleep.

I eased out of bed gently, careful not to wake her—I figured she deserved as much rest as she wanted. Still, my fingers itched to touch her naked back, to caress the exposed skin that I knew was soft as silk, but I resisted. Instead, I got dressed and headed to the kitchen. Munchkin followed me. After I put the coffee on, I took him for a quick walk before starting on breakfast.

There wasn't much to work with, but I had enough of the basics on hand to whip up some sausage and pancakes, which I knew Emzee would like. It had always been her go-to order on those rare occasions we'd made it to McDonald's before they stopped serving breakfast.

Pouring pancake batter onto the griddle, I thought more about the contrasts between Emzee and Claudia. The way, with Claudia, everything had been so rigidly routine.

Every day she'd wake up before me (sometimes even before the sun rose), turn on the coffee maker, and then lay out my agenda next to my cup. Even on the weekends, there'd be to-do lists or whole itineraries with museum visits or lunch plans detailed on them. Then she'd go work out. It was vitally important to her that she get her gym time in before the day started. I don't think I ever once saw her sleep in.

And breakfast? Claudia wasn't into it. She'd just choke down a quick protein shake on her way to the gym, even though she hated the chalky taste.

Lazy, mid-morning pancakes with Emzee could be nice. No stress. No rush. No lectures on the evils of various breakfast meats and their saturated fat content.

But of course, I couldn't let myself get used to it. My new wife didn't actually love me; she'd made that abundantly clear. So I wouldn't make the mistake of letting her fully into my life. Which was okay by me. After all, Claudia and I had gotten along just fine for years without being in love. It was when she started wanting more—when my parents started demanding more—that I'd realized I had to get out.

Obviously, I'd have to keep Emzee at a distance. Better for her, and better for me. The last thing either of us needed were entanglements that would make it any harder to end our marriage in a year. It seemed doubtful we'd be able to go back to the way things were before, but if we were lucky, we could remain in each other's lives. Maybe not as best friends, but I didn't like the idea of her disappearing completely.

Turning to set the platter of steaming pancakes on the table, I almost tripped over Munchkin, who'd apparently been sitting at my feet while I was cooking.

"You smell those sausages, boy?" I said. His stub of a tail wagged double-time, and I cut a piece for him to snack on while I was setting the table.

"You're spoiling him," Emzee scolded from the doorway, a smirk on her face. She still looked sleepy, but she'd put on a robe. The dog trotted over and rolled onto his back at her feet, and Em crouched down to give him a belly rub. "What a little mooch you are."

"Morning," I said. "I made brunch."

"It smells amazing," Emzee said, seating herself at the table. "Thank you."

After pouring us each a coffee and tuning the radio to an old-school jazz station, I sat down and we started eating. I could sense the tension between us, the weight of too many unspoken words. But I didn't know where to start.

The shoulder of her robe had slipped down a little, exposing that soft, bare skin, and part of me wanted to throw our breakfast in the sink, bend her over the table, and bang the shit out of her. To be honest, all I could think about was what we'd done last night. How wild she'd been when I took her on top of the desk. I'd expected her to balk at my cruelty, my roughness, but she seemed to love it. She'd been so fucking wet. She'd wanted me, wanted everything I'd given her. Just like she always did. I was getting hard at the thought.

When we were both done, Emzee put our dishes in the sink. It wasn't until she sat back down that she looked me straight in the eye.

"We need to talk," she said. "About last night."

I nodded. "I guess that was pretty weird. I'm sorry."

"No," she said. "It was fine."

"Just fine?" I raised an eyebrow.

Emzee blushed. "You know what I mean," she said. "It was kinky, but I was into it. I didn't dislike anything you did. It's just..."

Leaning forward, I coaxed, "Just what?"

She took a deep breath and then blurted, "I'm not interested in getting involved with whatever thoughts or feelings you have about Claudia."

"Em—" But she held up her hand before I could continue.

"We might not have an emotional relationship, but you still have to respect me. If you don't, we have to stop the sex, and I'll move into the guest room."

I let her words sink in, nodding slowly as I thought things over.

Maybe having her move into the guest room was the best thing for both of us. Because all that kink from last night? It had nothing to do with how I felt about Claudia, and everything to do with how I felt about Emzee. I wished *she* was the one who'd left her mark all over my apartment. That the stories I'd been telling had been about her instead.

I didn't like any of the memories that Claudia had left

behind. When I looked at that fucking Sri Lankan vase, all I thought about was how Claudia had spent half our trip bitching about the poverty there. How everything and everyone was so filthy and disgusting. Emzee never would have said that—she wouldn't have even thought it. If we'd been on that trip together, Emzee would have focused on observing the culture and people around her. She probably would have spent the whole trip taking photographs of everything: good, bad, or ugly.

To her, though, there would have been beauty in all of it.

And another thing—Emzee would never call all the miserable marriages in my family "traditional." Nor would she ever aspire to have a similar one for herself.

And that painting in the den? Emzee wouldn't have needed a fucking painting to remind her to communicate with her partner. She would just do it. Like she was doing now. Instead of pouting and acting passive-aggressive, the way Claudia always did when she was pissed at me for some reason or another.

And that desk. I knew for a fact that Em *most assuredly* would have been a lot more fun over drinks in Paris. All Claudia had wanted to do was shop on the Champs-Élysées and buy things that she could brag about to her friends. That was always all she ever cared about.

Not that it mattered anymore.

But even if Emzee and I did go to Paris or any of those other places now, it wouldn't change the fact that she didn't love me. That if I let her get inside me any more than she already had, I was going to break. Which was why I should agree to her terms. Call off the sex and let her move into the guest room.

Problem was, I couldn't do it. I was too selfish for that.

"I think it's for the best," Emzee was saying. "I can move all my stuff down the hall today. No one will have to know."

"No," I said.

She looked surprised. "No?"

"I can be respectful," I told her. "But as long as we're in this arrangement, you are my wife and you will sleep in my bed. Understood?"

Emzee scowled at me, but in the end, she didn't disagree.

I had to believe there was a part of her that didn't actually want to move into the guest room. Or that simply didn't want to give up our intense physical connection.

Either way, we'd reached a truce.

EMZEE

CHAPTER 10

It could get exhausting, trying to keep up the schedule for See Yourself. I *loved* the work I did—loved working with the ex-models, loved the classes I taught, loved knowing I was making a difference—but for the most part, all the behind-the-scenes logistics that went into making a nonprofit function tended to wear me out completely.

My main goal for the day had been to schedule the new guest instructors and classes for the next few months, but every time I called some rich and/or successful person who had expressed interest in volunteering with us, I was met with the exact same response.

"Oh, Emzee, it's such a great cause, and you know I truly, truly want to be involved, cross my heart, but it's just that I am so busy these days and..." Blah, blah, blah.

I nodded, even though I knew that Kendra couldn't see me. She was the latest socialite I'd called, who'd sworn just a few months ago that she'd be thrilled to give a presentation on how to perform well during job interviews—a life skill my students would obviously benefit from learning. And now this.

More excuses, more rejections, and a lot more panic on my part.

"Are you sure you can't make the time?" I asked, feeling a little desperate. "It's just a one-day seminar. Two to three hours, max."

"Let me see..."

I could practically hear her tapping her way through her calendar app.

"Maybe I could do something next month?" she said.

I pumped my fist with excitement. Kendra was one of the people I'd been counting on. She was a part-time recruiter for the most renowned makeup and fashion companies in the world, so she knew firsthand what made a resume sing or an interview crash and burn.

Flipping to next month's schedule, I said, "What about the ninth or the sixteenth?"

"Hmm. Oh. Wait," she said.

My pen drooped, and I braced myself for what was coming next.

"Gosh, it's just that I'm going to be in *Monte Carlo*," she said with a tragic sigh. "You understand, don't you? We'll have to reschedule when I get back."

"Sure," I said. "That'd be great."

After I hung up, I threw my desk calendar across the bedroom. I'd spent my entire morning on the phone with people like Kendra. People I'd met at galas or fundraisers or parties, who had expressed such genuine interest in See Yourself that I'd thought they would jump at the chance to be directly involved in shaping the future of these women.

Instead, whenever I called and tried to actually get them

on the schedule, they all had excuses. For Kendra it was Monte Carlo. For the Wirtzes, it had been the annual shareholders' meeting in Paris. Lily was in Tahiti "for the season," while Maddie's assistant informed me she was away filming a documentary on the homeless canine population in Athens.

None of them were available, but each of them had offered to write a check.

So, sure. I'd be happy to take their money. I couldn't in good faith turn down operating funds for the program, but at the same time, it wasn't what I needed. I needed *programming*. Gurus, educators, people who could help me and my students network. Not just open wallets.

After all, the whole point of the nonprofit was to teach these girls life skills with the help of actual mentors—but even when I got someone to agree to teach a class (which was rare enough), they tended to want to center *themselves* and focus more on how good they felt about offering their time, instead of the people I designed the organization to help. One husband and wife entrepreneurial team had even brought their own camera crew to record the class they taught, solely to be edited down and used in Instagram ads later.

Which I had allowed, because hey, more publicity.

But I was starting to feel like I was fighting an uphill battle. And I was doing it all alone.

I'd been in bed for hours with my calendar and my computer on my lap desk, trying to work. I couldn't use Ford's office, where the only available surface was the same desk we'd gotten down and dirty on top of. The desk he'd bought with Claudia in fucking Paris. There was no way I could've gotten any work done with all of that on my mind.

Setting my lap desk aside, I rolled over and face planted

on the bed, letting the bedding muffle my exasperated groans.

Of course, my husband chose that exact moment to wander in.

"What's going on?" he asked.

My head shot up, my hair—already in a haphazard bun on top of my head—flopping to the side. Ford was standing in the doorway of the bedroom, looking irritatingly casual and handsome as he ate an apple.

He probably never had problems with people promising things they would never deliver.

"I just wish people would actually keep their word," I said.

All the women I'd spoken with were acting like Claudia. It was exactly the kind of thing she would do—agree to volunteer because it made her feel good, and then when it was time to actually do the work, back out and write a check instead.

"Keep their word about what?" he asked.

"Just frustrating charity stuff," I said.

He frowned. "You're working on a Sunday?"

"I have to!" I said. "It's my nonprofit."

Walking over, he sat on the edge of the bed. Ever since he'd agreed to "respect" me, we'd managed to more or less keep our distance. As if there was this unspoken agreement that even though we were sleeping in the same bed, we shouldn't really touch each other.

"Talk to me," Ford said gently.

Because I was able to actually prioritize the ex-models—unlike *some* people—I launched into a brief description of my issues with the flaky socialite volunteer-wannabes without being catty or mentioning the Claudia comparison. An accomplishment of which I was quite proud.

After all, the last thing I wanted was to let on how pissy I still was about the whole Claudia thing.

"I just need someone—anyone—to come and teach a short, informative class on something career-related that would be useful for them in real life," I said.

I was racking my brain trying to think of who else I could call when Ford cleared his throat. "I'll do it," he said.

"Wait, what?"

"Why not?" he said. "I can talk to them about real estate and business in general—that would be helpful, right?"

For a moment I just stared at him, surprised and over-whelmed by gratitude.

"Honestly, that would be amazing."

"Cool. Let's set a date then," he said, pulling out his phone and looking at his calendar.

Unlike anyone else I'd dealt with all day, I had Ford written into the schedule in seconds—and then confirmed via pinkie swear. It immediately put me in a better mood.

It also seemed to dissolve any lingering tension between me and Ford, to the point that after I'd put my laptop away, I felt like I could hang out with him almost normally.

Over the next few days, we finally started getting into a daily routine as a couple. We were figuring out how to live together, taking turns with chores and meals, learning each other's rhythms. His apartment even began to feel more like home. And our relationship solidified, in a sense—not into a real marriage exactly, but more like how it used to be. Comforting and safe.

We woke up around the same time, though Ford got ready for the day a lot quicker than I did. Because of that, he'd usually go to the kitchen and feed Munchkin before making coffee for us. I'd always started my day with a meal, but eating a solid breakfast was apparently a bit of a new concept for Ford. Still, he took to it readily, and we'd take turns cooking.

I figured out pretty quickly that he liked his eggs with cheese scrambled into them, and I noticed that he quietly changed to turkey bacon after I mentioned my preference for it. We'd sit there eating companionably each morning, secretly feeding Munchkin the crusts of our toast under the table, both of us pretending we weren't.

Afterward, we'd catch up on emails while we finished our coffee, and then head out to our separate offices (or my loft, if I had a photoshoot lined up). For the majority of our waking hours, we conducted our lives completely apart, with minimal communication.

We had a dinner routine as well. Neither of us were much for cooking, so we usually just got takeout, picked up by whoever was going to get home the latest. Whoever got home first would set the wine to breathing.

We'd eat and drink and talk about work or my nonprofit, and then we'd take Munchkin out for his evening walk. Once we were in bed, we'd revert to beast mode, fucking each other senseless, but the next day we would act like it had never happened.

All in all, my married life was fun and easy and simple.

We didn't mention our problems, and we especially didn't talk about sex—and how it was starting to feel more and more like the only place where we could really share our feelings without any words at all. At least, that was how it felt for me.

Right now, it was the best I could hope for.

EMZEE

CHAPTER 11

I t was my first Vault Lunch with The Wives since I'd gotten back from the honeymoon. I was eager to see my sisters-in-law and catch up, but also a little nervous. I knew that having lunch with them would require some measure of playing pretend.

Everything had changed since our last ladies' outing... and at the same time, nothing had. Because regardless of the devil's bargain I'd made with the senior Malones to make the Bratva go away (which had to remain a secret from *everyone*), I was still so in love with Ford that it hurt. And I was pretty sure he was still in love with Claudia. I'd never escape her shadow.

Day to day, I'd been able to keep up a front of not caring about the true state of my marriage—and ignoring the countdown to the divorce I'd agreed to—but I had my doubts that I'd succeed in such subterfuge around Tori and Brooklyn. Those two were like bloodhounds. They'd know something was up, something beyond the fact of the marriage being a joint deception by me and my husband.

Not only that, but the nice, new normal that Ford and I

had established was something that I cherished. Going to lunch with my sisters would pop the happy little bubble of normalcy we'd created. Some selfish part of me wished I could just cancel on them and continue living in my fantasy version of reality.

But no. That would only make things harder for me later. May as well get my heart thrashed as often as possible. Remind myself not to get too attached to the lie.

Luckily, with Tori's due date so close, I knew the focus wouldn't be on me for long.

"I still can't believe I'm going to be an aunt!" I crowed after we'd ordered.

We were at Jiao, prepared to stuff ourselves silly with every variety of perfectly cooked Chinese dumpling, spicy kimchee, and crunchy, vinegary-sweet cucumber salad.

"I know," Tori said, rubbing her stomach. "Stefan is so excited, he's barely slept."

"How are you feeling?" I asked her. "Besides excited-slash-nervous, I mean."

She smiled. "I feel great, actually. I'm ready. Ready to have this little girl in my arms and ready to be not-pregnant anymore. I can't wait to meet her."

"Awww," Brooklyn and I cooed. The feeling was mutual.

"And how was St. Barts?" Brooklyn asked, turning to me. "I want all the details. Especially the sexy ones."

Her baby bump was more noticeable now, and like Tori, she seemed to constantly, reflexively touch her stomach.

"It was love at first sight," I sighed, the memories coming back full force. "So pretty, and so relaxing—way less of a party vibe than our Bahamas trip. And the beaches are *incredible*. White sand, clear water, and we had the most amazing weather. Did you know they have wild iguanas just crawling around everywhere?"

"That is so cool," Tori said. "Did you take advantage of the touristy stuff? Snorkeling?"

"Yep," I said. "And we went windsurfing almost every day. And the food!"

"Maybe Luka and I should plan a trip there before the baby comes," Brooklyn mused. "I heard there are nude beaches. Did you two check any of those out?" She winked at me.

"Um, and our private villa was the best," I said, anxious to change the subject. "Here, I have tons of pictures saved on my phone. You can see for yourselves. Look at that infinity pool."

As they oohed and ahhed, the waiter returned with our food. Just as we started to dig in, Brooklyn's phone buzzed in her purse.

"I'm so sorry, let me just check that real quick," she said. "I've been waiting to hear back from the caterers for Tor's baby shower."

Jumping on the opportunity to get their minds on something besides my personal life, I finished chewing a dreamy truffle and beef dumpling and said, "Speaking of, we should probably talk logistics for the party, yes?"

With that, the conversation completely moved away from me. There was plenty to discuss—who was doing what, where it would be, who was invited.

It seemed almost as involved as planning a wedding.

We spent the rest of the lunch focusing on making a list of all the things we needed to do, dividing responsibilities between myself and Brooklyn, and picking a theme.

"Something cute," Tori said. "Colorful. And not just pink everywhere. Are there any more tofu and mushroom?"

I passed her the requested dumplings, took out my phone, and began browsing Pinterest for ideas.

"Winnie the Pooh?" I suggested.

Tori wrinkled her nose and shook her head. "I feel like we should avoid anything involving 'pooh' for as long as we can."

We all laughed.

"How about a woodland theme?" I suggested as I continued scrolling. "With animals."

"That's cute," Tori said. "I like that direction."

"I love that," Brooklyn agreed. "And I'll bet one of the botanical gardens has a pretty tea room type space we can rent, with lots of plants and greenery. It will be adorable."

"Oooh, look at these cute fox face cupcakes!" I said, showing them my screen. "And these porcupine cheese logs."

Brooklyn was writing everything down. "I know exactly the right bakery to call," she said. "We can get the decorations on Etsy. Maybe lean into the *Fantastic Mr. Fox* vibes?"

"Yes!" Tori's eyes were sparkling. "Just don't go too crazy—I'd love something small and intimate, maybe a dozen or so guests."

"Not me," Brooklyn said. "When it's my turn, I want the biggest, loudest, most Instagram-worthy baby shower ever. Piles of confetti and flowers and balloons. Hint, hint."

I laughed. "We can make that work. One baby shower at a time, though."

She and Tori exchanged a look, and then smiled at me with a conspiratorial gleam in their eyes. My stomach sank a little.

"What?"

"It's just, well..." Tori looked at Brooklyn and then back at me. "I'm pregnant. Brooklyn's pregnant."

"Yes, and?" I asked.

"I guess we're just thinking...that you'll be next," Brooklyn said teasingly.

Everything seemed to freeze in that moment. I'd done so well ignoring all the real feelings I had for Ford. Allowing myself to settle into a simple routine with him, one that kept my heart safe, keeping in mind the impending divorce and the fact that our marriage could never become something more than a ruse. And now this.

"Oh no," I said, forcing a laugh. "We're both too focused on our careers right now to even *think* about getting pregnant."

With horror, I realized I was parroting Ford's parents, and I gulped down my jasmine tea to cover my frown.

"Still. It can happen when you least expect it," Brooklyn said.

"Plus we're way too young," I said.

"I mean," Tori said with a grin, "I'm younger than you are, Em."

"Honestly, it's just too soon for us," I tried again. "A baby is a lot to think about."

I wasn't prepared for this topic to be on the table.

Somehow, I managed to put on a happy face and redirect the conversation back to Tori's baby shower, but inside I was secretly imagining what it would be like to have a baby with Ford.

Would it have his chin, and those deep dimples I loved? My gray eyes and shyness? I couldn't help thinking about how cute it could be, a baby Ford/Emzee. A Fordzee.

I'd never thought of myself as motherly—especially since I'd missed out on the whole mothering experience that most people got—but now that the idea was in my head, I could almost picture it. It made my chest feel tight and my heart warm.

Because it wasn't just a baby I wanted to share with Ford. I wanted a whole life. No matter how much I kept telling myself that I could make it through this next year without getting too attached, I hadn't realized how much it would hurt to deny myself the things I really wanted. Which was a real life, and a real marriage. I wanted everything my sisters had.

I realized then that Tori and Brooklyn really did feel like my sisters. Even though I couldn't tell them absolutely everything that was going on with me.

God, I wished I could just let down my guard and be real with them. Spill the whole truth about Ford, and the Bratva, and the horrible but necessary deal I'd made with Ford's parents. But if I told them about the Bratva's threats, I'd be betraying my brothers, especially Stefan, to whom I'd promised secrecy.

This bargain I'd made with the Malones was my opportunity to save our family. To protect my brothers, their wives, and their unborn babies.

It was what I wanted.

But I couldn't deny the twinge in my heart at the thought of having a baby with Ford. Or the desire to turn to my sisters and say, "Hell yes, I'm totally next. Ford and I are going to start trying right away."

Instead, I had to lie to them. I had to smile and lie and deflect. It was becoming second nature.

Would there ever come a time when I didn't have to lie to everyone I cared about?

EMZEE

CHAPTER 12

Pacing the lobby of the building where Danica Rose Management's offices were, I told myself not to be nervous. Jorge, the head of security, gave me a nod each time I passed the reception desk, but it didn't do much to calm me. I couldn't help worrying that Ford would be a disappointment.

Yes, he'd said that he would come and teach a workshop for See Yourself, and yes, we'd confirmed the day and time and we'd even talked about it this morning over breakfast... but there was a part of me that wasn't entirely sure he wouldn't let me down.

The fact was, everyone else who'd agreed to help with the nonprofit had found a way to back out at the last minute, and they were all from the same world that Ford was. It was hard not to be wary. In my experience, those who occupied the highest social and economic circles could be a bit lacking in the area of personal responsibility. And although things had been going well with Ford lately, there was no guarantee that he'd come through.

I checked my delicate Shinola watch for about the

hundredth time and smoothed down the front of my skirt—
my favorite black pencil skirt that usually helped me feel
powerful and in control—and resisted the urge to call Ford
and demand a status report. After all, he wasn't even
supposed to be here for at least another twenty minutes, but
that didn't make me any less neurotic. My girls were
counting on this seminar.

Before I could complete another circuit of the lobby,
Ford came strolling into the building, looking absolutely
delicious in a dark suit with a charcoal patterned tie. As
Jorge took Ford's ID to get him checked in, my husband's
eyes focused on me.

"What's wrong? Did you think I'd bail?" he asked.

"No!" I lied. "I'm just...excited. Why don't I show you
up to the conference room?"

He nodded, but I caught his eyes wandering down the
length of my body. It seemed that he liked the way my skirt
hugged my curves. I couldn't help thinking he would probably like it a whole lot more if it was shoved up around my
waist.

"Lead the way," he said, a wolfish gleam in his eyes.

We stepped into the elevator and suddenly Ford was all
business, going over all the main points he'd be covering in
his presentation. "It runs just under an hour long, and then
I figured I'd just take as many questions as we have time
for."

"Sounds perfect," I said.

The doors dinged open and we stepped into DRM's
offices. Ford frowned a little as I led him down the hall
toward the large conference room I'd reserved.

"Do you not worry that some of the women might have
a hard time being here?" he asked, glancing around. "I
mean, with everything that happened before...with your

father, and the agency...I don't know, maybe they'd have some kind of post-traumatic stress?"

I nodded, impressed that he'd given the issue some real thought.

"That's actually the whole reason I hold most of our classes over at the studio space nearby. But it doesn't have the audio-visual setup that we need today, and since you're speaking about business, it seemed the more appropriate venue.

"Don't worry, though—the email I sent out specifically mentioned that we'd be in the agency's offices for your seminar, and I called all the girls who signed up to confirm that they were comfortable with the location. So we're good to go."

"That was smart of you," Ford said. "And compassionate."

I felt my stomach do a little twist at the compliments. "Thanks. And here we are."

After I opened the door, I gestured for him to enter first.

The conference room was mostly ready, with a projector and a screen and some cables laid out so Ford could plug in his laptop and get started. As he set up, clicking through a few files and getting his PowerPoint open, I took a seat in the far corner and set down my bag.

"We have water, but do you want me to grab you a coffee before the girls arrive?" I said.

"Thanks, but I'm properly caffeinated for the day," he said, and then seemed to notice my bag and notebook on the chair. "Are you staying for the whole thing?"

"Yes," I said. "Is that a problem?"

"Why, Mrs. Malone," he said, smiling. "Do you not trust me to run this workshop?"

"Why, Mr. Malone," I responded. "Do you think this

program would have survived after the very first guest lecture if I didn't sit in?"

It wasn't just that I was there to keep the speaker on track—there was always the very real concern that some of my girls might have a hard time relaxing with a man in charge of the room and only other models around. Choosing a safe venue was only half the battle. After all, the male power dynamic was exactly what had harmed most of these ex-models in the not-too-distant past. My goal was to help them, not put them in situations where it would be difficult for them to focus and therefore succeed.

Everyone knew this wasn't a Jeffrey Epstein/Ghislaine Maxwell situation, that I wasn't grooming them to be passed off to someone like my father—they knew I would do everything in my power to keep them safe. But that also meant I was often a bit overprotective.

I didn't care. I would fight to the death to keep them feeling safe.

Which also meant I was going to give Ford a little talking-to.

Because as much as I didn't want to bring down the mood, I knew what an incorrigible flirt my husband could be. I couldn't think of a time I'd seen him interact with a woman without pouring on the charm. It didn't matter if she was a fresh faced co-ed or a grandmother with a dozen grandkids. Ford saw a female and instantly turned on the charm.

That wouldn't work here. He couldn't flirt with the girls. He couldn't give off any kind of sexually charged dynamic.

"So listen. I just want to reiterate that they've been through a lot," I said, walking over to him. "And some of them are uncomfortable around men. It's one of the reasons I prefer to have women teach the workshops."

Ford nodded. "I get it. Really."

"Good," I said, relieved. "I just want you to understand where the girls are coming from."

He nodded again, but before we could talk more, the door to the conference room opened and the girls began trickling in. They smiled at me, but when they saw Ford, I noticed a few of their smiles faltering.

I glanced over at Ford, whose own smile had dimmed a bit. He'd noticed their change in attitude when they'd seen him.

Sitting down at the back of the room, I was nervous all over again. I held my breath as Ford introduced himself.

"I have to thank my lovely wife, Emzee, for inviting me to come in today and teach you all about real estate," he said. "Do you mind if I turn off the lights? It'll be easier to see the PowerPoint, and I'll turn them back on afterward so you can read the hand-outs I brought."

The women nodded, and I could sense them loosening up a little already.

I was impressed. Not just by Ford asking permission, but with the tone of his voice as well as his demeanor. I hadn't been sure he'd really heard what I was saying, but wow.

There was absolutely no flirtation in his words, none of the usual winking or banter. My playboy husband was stepping up, 100% professional, treating the women around the conference table as seriously as he would treat any man.

The lights went down, and as Ford talked us through his background, his job, and all the ins and outs of real estate development, I found myself riveted. Not just by what he was teaching, but by how he delivered it. And he was calm, approachable, and thoughtful in responding to questions. I even asked a few myself to keep the ball rolling.

After he was done and the lights came up, he passed around packets that contained notes and resources and other helpful information. When I got mine, he flashed me a small smile, but by the time he was back at the front of the room he was all business again.

"So let's go over a typical career path, and bear in mind that not all real estate is about commercial or residential development—some of you may be interested in becoming an agent, helping people find their first home or working with a restaurant owner seeking new locations."

He spoke with authority, but not aggression. The eye contact he offered came with brief frowns of concentration, not little winks of acknowledgement, and he paid no more attention to any one attendee than he did to any other. In fact, the only time I saw even a hint of the flirtatious Ford that I knew was when he'd walk over every so often to give me a big grin or a shoulder squeeze that everyone could see.

It felt good to bask in his light, but I'd almost forgotten how sexy it could be to bask in it whilst in public.

As he started to wrap up, I realized I was practically squirming in my chair. All the intelligence and tips and authentic displays of helpfulness that Ford had showed during the seminar had me more hot and bothered than I could have ever imagined.

By the time the last questions had been answered, I was just about ready to bone my husband right there in the conference room.

Ford concluded his talk to a round of applause. As the women filed out, he handed each of them his business card and told them they could reach out if they had any more questions. Once we were alone again, I closed the door and quietly locked it.

When I turned back to Ford, he was packing up his computer, completely oblivious to the way I was staring at him. Like he was a five-course meal and I was starving.

Luckily, I'd reserved the conference room for two full hours. We still had it for another fifteen minutes.

My entire body was buzzing with desire as I pushed away from the door and stalked toward him, unbuttoning my blouse as I did. By the time Ford looked up, my shirt was open to my navel and my cleavage was showing, plumped up above my black lace bra.

He did a double take, and then his smile morphed into the wolfish one I knew so well.

"Why, Mrs. Malone," he said, turning and crossing his arms as he leaned back on the desk. "Are you trying to seduce me?"

"I don't know, Mr. Malone," I said, finishing with my shirt and opening it wide so he could see that the black lace was see-through. "Are you looking to be seduced?"

It was a question I didn't really need to ask. When I reached him, he grabbed me by the waist and spun me around to face the conference table, his hard cock pressed up against my ass. His hands slid over the tight stretch of my skirt before going down to the hem.

"Is this what you want?" he demanded.

I spread my hands on the table, arching my back. "Yes," I hissed.

"You're a dirty girl," he said, but I could hear the heat and delight in his voice.

"We have less than fifteen minutes," I said.

"I can make you come in five."

His confidence only made me hotter, and by the time he

got my skirt up past my hips, my underwear was soaked through. Ford let out a groan when he realized it.

"Did you like my class?" he asked, running his finger along the fabric, touching me, teasing me, but not giving me any of the relief I was dying for.

"Yes," I moaned as his other hand came forward to cup my breast, which was practically spilling out of my balconette bra.

His thumb and forefinger pinched my nipple, and I gripped the table with anticipation as I listened to him unzip his pants. I was waiting for him to slide my panties off, but instead he just pulled them to the side as he rubbed the tip of his cock against my hot, ready pussy.

"Ford," I moaned. "Hurry."

"You want this cock?" he whispered, his voice in my ear.

I nodded, loving the feel of him stretched out on top of me, of being pressed down against the cool surface of the table, my hips braced against the edge.

"Were you paying attention in class? Or were you thinking about my cock? About me fucking you here, at work, where anyone could walk in and see us?"

All I could manage was a breathy moan.

"You're going to have to be quiet," he warned me. "Very, very quiet."

I'd never considered myself an exhibitionist before, but I was starting to realize that I really, really liked it when we had sex in a place where we might get caught.

Even though I'd locked the door, there was always the possibility that someone could walk by and hear us. And it was going to be very, very hard to be quiet with Ford teasing me mercilessly with his cock.

He was right there, brushing up against my entrance

but refusing to fill me up the way he knew I desperately wanted him to.

"Tell me you were thinking about me," Ford demanded.

"I was thinking about you," I gasped.

He pushed forward, just a little bit, just the head of his cock slipping inside me.

"Come on, Em," he said. "You can do better than that."

"Please," I begged, my voice hoarse. "Please fuck me, Mr. Malone."

With a groan, Ford sank deep inside me, filling me up, stretching me. My head went back and I bit my lip to keep from crying out. It felt so good. So naughty and dangerous and perfect.

My underwear was still drawn to the side, but Ford gripped the silky fabric in his hand and used it to rub my clit. The sweet, slick pressure was too much and soon I was muffling my cries with my hand.

Ford began fucking me harder, faster, whispering dirty nothings in my ear, clearly doing his best to make good on his promise to make me come in five minutes.

It only took three.

EMZEE

CHAPTER 13

Cocktail parties were probably my least favorite way to spend an evening. I'd have to get my hair done, my nails done, take at least an hour to do my makeup and decide what to wear, and then spend the entire night in what was usually a too-tight dress and too-high heels trying to make small talk with people I didn't know. Not the most comfortable environment for me.

Honestly, I'd much rather stay at home in my coziest pajamas, watching a movie on the couch with Munchkin and a full glass of wine.

But tonight's shindig was a work event for Ford. It was one of those "schmooze a bunch of high-dollar investors" types of parties. The kind of thing he loved. And since he'd stepped in where *he* wasn't comfortable—teaching that real estate class for See Yourself, helping mentor my girls—I owed it to him to be the consummate plus one. His help had meant a lot to me, and I was happy to return the favor. And maybe receive an equal reward for myself afterward...

Besides all that, I was his wife. Fake or not, it was my

job to be at his side for stuff like this. So I did what I had to do.

Went to the salon to get a fuss-free updo, consisting of a blow-out followed by a sleek ponytail, got my nails done in a nice, respectable neutral beige. I did my makeup, nothing too fancy, and even traded my go-to black liquid liner for a subtler dark brown.

Then I picked a dress: a black Kate Spade sheath with an open triangle in the back. It wasn't too showy, but it was definitely sexy, with cap sleeves and a hemline that hit just above the knee. After some deliberation, I paired it with my Jimmy Choo stilettos that made my short legs look a mile long. Grabbing my trusty Prada clutch, I checked myself out in the mirror.

Hot. Ford would appreciate the outfit, especially my exposed back.

But when it was time to leave for the party, he barely paid attention to me. He didn't comment once on how I looked, or the effort I'd put into my appearance. And when we arrived at the ritzy art gallery where the event was being held, he beelined over to some short guy in a suit and seemed to forget I was even there.

I mean, I understood. To an extent. It was a work event. He had to put his best professional foot forward, not spend the evening flirting with his wife.

Yet as I stood in a corner, trying to look like I was happy to be there, I couldn't help wondering why I'd been invited in the first place. Ford certainly didn't need any help working the room, judging by the looks of it.

Wasn't he aware how difficult it was for me to feel alone and abandoned in a crowd—especially one consisting of loud, wealthy investor types? Ford, of all people, should know precisely how anxious social events made me. Seeing as how he was the one who swooped in to rescue me when I was living the life of a permanent, solo wallflower in high school.

Fifteen minutes in, I'd had enough. Pity party over. If Ford wanted me to stand around by myself for a few hours, I would handle it. I'd been forced to endure worse. Time for a drink.

I went to the bar to get a glass of red wine, which I brought back to my corner and nursed slowly, trying to keep a pleasant, neutral expression on my face. At least I was by the door where the waiters came out with their trays of crab cakes, so I was always right there to get a fresh one.

I'd probably eaten half a dozen and was just about to reach the bottom of my wineglass when I was joined by a tall, sandy-haired man with a friendly smile. He looked around my age, and he was handsome. Not knee-weakeningly so, like Ford—more of a bland, All-American kind of handsome, in the way of rich young men who wore Ralph Lauren and owned boats or horses.

"Hi," he said, holding out a hand.

"Hello," I said politely, quickly wiping my crab-cakey fingers on a napkin before I accepted his handshake.

"I'm Andrew."

"Emzee," I said.

"I couldn't help noticing you all alone over here," he said with that nice smile of his.

I flushed, embarrassed that a perfect stranger had noticed that I was basically hiding in a corner during a party.

"I'm just taking a breather from the crowd," I said.

Which wasn't a complete lie. I *was* taking a break...from the pressure to perform in a situation where I felt out of place and uncomfortable.

"Understandable," he said. "It can get a little overwhelming." He glanced over my shoulder. "And you definitely found the best place to hide. First dibs on the crab cakes."

"They are pretty fantastic," I admitted, feeling caught out.

Andrew gave me a wink. "It's a good thing they don't have shrimp cocktail tonight. Those are my weakness. I can put away ten, maybe twelve of them at a party like this. It's pretty horrifying—for me and anyone else that's watching."

I laughed. It was hard not to like the guy. He was nice and funny, and he was putting me at ease. After he fetched us a fresh round of drinks, I thought to myself that maybe the evening wouldn't be so bad after all.

"This is a really nice venue," he observed, looking around the gallery.

"It is," I agreed.

That was the one good thing about this event. Malone Real Estate Holdings had booked out a very well-known, highly respected art gallery. I'd heard good things about their latest exhibit, so I'd been looking forward to the location, if not the actual event. But once Ford and I had arrived, it became obvious that no one was really interested in what was hanging on the walls. And the room was a bit too crowded to get any good views of the photos on display.

But what I'd seen, I'd liked.

"I really like the curation," he said. "Not that I can see much of the art in this crowd."

It was as if he'd read my mind. I looked at him, startled.

"What?" he asked, mistaking my expression for something else. "Oh God, please don't tell me you're the photographer and this is exactly the kind of event where you feel your work is best displayed."

I laughed again. "No, no, no," I reassured him. "I'm not the photographer. I like the work as well. I was actually just thinking the same thing."

"Ah. So which one is your favorite?" he asked. "Of what you can see."

I glanced around, trying to reacquaint myself with the work I'd attempted to check out when I first arrived. I didn't know the photographer, but I was impressed with what I saw. Lots of beautiful architecture, mostly in and around Chicago it seemed, but shot from unique angles and perspectives that made it look more like abstract art than photographs.

"I think I like that one the best," I said, pointing to one across the room.

It was the skyline of our city, familiar and iconic, but captured from above in a grid pattern of shadows and shapes. I found it evocative and interesting.

"The artist has a gift for playing with light and dark to emphasize form," I said. "And I can't help noticing the care they seem to take with the negative spaces."

Now it was Andrew who was giving me a surprised look.

"What?" I asked, feeling self-conscious.

"Nothing," he said, smiling broadly. "I just don't meet many people at these events who care much about art, let alone the specifics of form and negative space. I'm impressed."

"Well, I do have a background in the arts."

His eyebrows went up and I could sense his interest shifting completely over to me. I wasn't used to getting this kind of attention at parties. I knew he was flirting a little, which would probably bother Ford, but it seemed harmless. It wasn't like I was flirting back.

I was simply bored, and Andrew was nice, and he was interested in art and photography like me. So far, he was the only person at this event who had made me feel like I belonged.

"So you *are* a photographer," he said. "My assumption was half correct, then."

Nodding, I admitted, "I mostly do commercial work for my family's company, Danica Rose Management."

His interest became even more obvious. "The modeling agency?"

"That's right." I hoped he didn't know too much about the reputation we'd had before we switched our name and our brand. We were all still working hard to overcome the ugly notoriety our father had brought down on the Zoric name.

"You all put up some great billboards downtown recently," he said. "I don't suppose you had a hand in that campaign?"

"Actually, yeah. I shot all of those images," I said. "I was promoted to a broader creative role a few months ago, so I basically ran point on the whole campaign."

It had been intended as a relaunch of sorts—moving away from my father's branding of the agency as a literal collection of the most beautiful women in the world, and toward an image that was edgy, artistic, and inclusive. My brothers had been happy to put me in charge.

Andrew let out a low whistle. "They're lucky to have you."

"It's my job. Not that I don't love the work I do for DRM. It's just...I don't know."

"Just what?" he prompted with a playful look. "Tell me."

"Sometimes I wish I could get away," I confessed. "Step

back from the family business and take a little time to do some projects of my own. I've had gallery shows, shot for *National Geographic*, but it's been a while. Commercial photography can be a little mercenary."

Andrew nodded. "So you're smart *and* ambitious. I like that."

I'd never been called ambitious before. My family appreciated the work I did, and I knew that Ford was supportive as well, but I sometimes got the sense that everyone thought of my photography as more of a hobby than a long-term career. Maybe that was why I'd been able to confess my feelings to Andrew, basically a complete stranger, before anyone in my family.

The thing was, I couldn't just abandon ship to go off on some self-indulgent, soul-searching art sabbatical. As much as I yearned to photograph the wider world—I loved visiting ancient ruins and crumbling cemeteries in particular—I had a responsibility to make sure the agency and all the people it employed stayed afloat.

Still, it was nice to talk about my dreams with someone.

"I'd love to see more of your work sometime," he said. "Outside of the agency stuff."

"Okay?" I said, a little surprised by his interest. "Sure. I mean, I'm flattered."

He took his wallet out, extracted a business card, and handed it over. "I have to confess, I'm not just a casual observer. I'm in the business myself, so to speak."

Andrew Apellido, Editor-in-Chief, *lookingglass*.

"We're an up-and-coming online publication," he said. "I've seen your work, and I have to say, you've got just the eye. I think you're perfect for what we're looking for. Plus, if you don't mind me saying so, the Zoric name would be a good prestige boost for the magazine."

I didn't mind, especially since a lot of people still saw my family as pariahs. It was nice to know others out there still thought the Zoric name carried some weight. In a good way.

Then I turned over the card and noticed the address. "Oh."

"What?" Andrew asked. "Did I say something wrong?"

"No," I said. "It's just that you're based in New York. I mean, I know the internet is a thing, but—"

"Ah. Yes," he said. "I'd want you there in person. Ideally, we'd send you out on freelance assignments, eventually giving you more creative control—maybe even a permanent position if it works out. I'd love to discuss it more in detail. We could fly you out, of course."

I found myself tempted. What would it be like to go to New York to work? To move there? I'd miss my family, for sure, but maybe I deserved a fresh start. If it weren't for Ford, I'd probably say yes.

But my chest hurt when I remembered that he wouldn't be in my way forever. That our marriage was temporary.

Clearing the tightness from my throat, I said, "Circle back to me in a year. I've got a contract I can't get out of, but I'm interested. For sure."

He looked pleased. "Why don't I give you my personal number. That way you can call me directly once your contract is up."

We exchanged our contact info, and just as Andrew was finishing up entering his number into my phone, Ford appeared out of the crowd.

The expression on his face was one I'd never seen before. He looked like a caveman, stalking aggressively toward us, his eyes shifting between me and Andrew. When he reached me, he put his arm around my waist, pulling me close.

Definitely caveman behavior.

"Ford," I said, trying to smooth things over. "This is Andrew Apellido. He's the editor-in-chief of a magazine in New York."

"Oh?" Ford gave Andrew a glare, lifting his hand to stroke my shoulder possessively.

"We were talking about *work* opportunities," I said pointedly.

"Is that so," Ford said, sounding skeptical.

I didn't like my husband's tone. I didn't like his meat-headed show of ownership over me. And I really didn't like how rude he was being to Andrew.

"This is my husband, Ford Malone," I said to Andrew, hoping he would understand.

"Pleasure to meet you," Andrew said coolly, giving Ford a terse nod.

He responded with, "I appreciate you keeping my wife company while I was busy. I can take it from here." So dismissive. Like he was just shooing Andrew away.

Seriously? I'd been standing around by myself all night, but of course, this is what finally got Ford's attention. Another man chatting me up. I shot Andrew a look that I hoped expressed my apology for my husband's behavior.

"Emzee," Andrew said with a gentle smile. "It was lovely meeting you and having a chance to talk about art. I hope we'll connect again soon. Ford—"

"Goodbye," Ford said pointedly, with a condescending smile on his face.

Andrew raised a brow, and I felt Ford go tense next to me.

Thankfully, Andrew excused himself before my husband could make a scene.

Still, the damage had been done. I was beyond humiliated at my husband's behavior.

As soon as Andrew was out of sight, I shrugged off Ford's arm and walked away.

FORD

CHAPTER 14

What the hell had happened at the party?

As I drove us home, tense and silent, all I could do was replay the events of the night in my head, over and over again, trying to figure out when—and how—everything had turned to such shit.

Emzee and I had walked into the gallery, which I knew for a fact she'd been excited to check out, and the first person we ran into had been my colleague Xavier from the Malone Real Estate offices across town. After chatting for a minute, I'd turned to formally introduce my wife, only to find that she'd disappeared. Which was a little awkward for me, sure, but I figured she'd just been so excited about the photography on display that she had slipped away to check it out.

I'd never had a problem flying solo at schmooze-fests such as these, so I'd taken off on my own to begin my rounds with the guests—assuming Emzee would catch up with me once she'd soaked in some of the art.

Which had reminded me, I really owed her a proper date of some kind. Newlyweds went on dates, didn't they?

Someplace cool but cultured, where Em could scratch that artistic itch of hers, get fired up about light and shadow and all that. I knew what she liked.

Soon enough, I was in the thick of it all. In my element. At some point, I guess I got so caught up in the socializing that I lost track of time, because suddenly I checked my Breitling and it was an hour later and Emzee was still conspicuously MIA. To the point where I was getting annoyed at having to make excuses for her absence to everyone who inquired about my new wife. Not to mention all the roasting I endured, the jokes about how she must be sick of being married to me already. Ha fucking ha.

And then I'd heard Emzee's laugh. That infectious, irrepressible laugh of hers, ringing out clear across the room. It froze me in my tracks, and I spun toward the sound with a smile already on my face—only to be met with the infuriating sight of my wayward wife, mid-flirt. Huddled in a corner mere inches away from some mouth-breathing New Yorker.

Fucking Andrew Apellido. Who did this guy he think he was?

It was obvious what had been on his mind while he'd been cozying up to Emzee. Even from across the room, his body language was unmistakable. He wanted her. And it had nothing to do with her photography, no matter what Emzee had tried to tell me. That asshole had been standing there undressing my wife with his eyes, getting off on presenting himself as someone who could actually help her career. I knew the type all too well.

Not that I could blame him for trying. Even in a plain black dress and heels, Emzee was a total fucking knockout. Her tits looked distractingly plump in that tight dress, and the heels she wore made me want to wrap her legs around my neck. I'd spent most of the night trying not to think about pulling her into some empty back room, shoving her dress up to her hips and fucking her over a table the way I'd done in the conference room at DRM.

That had been a hot, yet pleasant surprise. I'd never expected my shy wife to come on to me at her office, and I definitely hadn't expected her to be so into it.

"You gonna text Andrew as soon as we get home?" I asked, glancing over at her.

Emzee didn't say a word, remaining as silent and sullen as she'd been ever since I had pulled her out of the gallery and told her we were going home early.

"You know why he gave you his number, right?" I ribbed. I couldn't help myself. The scumbag had gotten under my skin. "It's not just a job that he's hoping to give you."

She turned her head farther toward the window, and I could see that her hands were balled up into fists. Guess she was even more furious than I'd thought. I'd been hoping we could just bang it out once we got home, but as I turned into the parking structure of my building, she let out an angry huff, and I realized she wasn't going to just spontaneously get over the bug that had crawled up her ass. She was obviously spoiling for a fight.

Or worse—a Talk.

Emzee started up the moment we were alone in the elevator.

"Your behavior tonight was completely unacceptable."

"My behavior?" I scoffed.

"Yes."

I couldn't believe what I was hearing. *My* behavior was unacceptable? Okay, so maybe I'd been a little possessive when I first went over to her, but how else was I supposed to react to seeing my wife yucking it up with that sleazy piece of garbage?"

"What about *yours*?" I shot back. "How do you think it looks for my wife to be cozying up to another man?"

The look on her face had me stepping back. We arrived at our floor and had barely gotten through the door of the apartment before Emzee was at my throat again.

"Although it's flattering that you assume any conversation I'm having with a man involves him trying to hook up with me, it's also incredibly insulting," she seethed. "*Networking is conversation.* Professional circles involve men and women conversing together all the time. Often over drinks! You can't act like a petty jealous husband every time that happens. Because it *will* happen. We're supposed to be a power couple, right? That implies that we *both* have power. Reputations. Careers."

Even though her face was red when she finished, I couldn't help admiring how passionately she'd argued her case. Not that I thought she was right.

"Yeah, yeah," I said. "But I don't see why you thought it needed to happen at *my* event. When you're a power couple, you support each other. You should have been on my arm."

I felt like a caveman, trying to explain myself but feeling frustrated and upset at how Emzee seemed to be slipping away before my eyes. And right when things were starting to get good between us, when we'd found a rhythm and a schedule that kept our lives copacetic.

"You bailed on me the second we walked into that party," I went on. "Do you have any idea how much shit I got from my colleagues for having a runaway wife?"

"This is about your dumb male pride?" Emzee narrowed her eyes.

"No," I said. "It's about you showing up for me. Which apparently you aren't all that interested in, when it comes right down to it."

Munchkin had barreled into the room in the midst of our fighting, and now he was anxiously prancing at our feet, letting out pathetic little whines of distress. Emzee crouched down to soothe him before straightening up to her full (but minimal) height again.

"Firstly, I *tried* to be on your arm," she said, scowling. "But you ignored me. I don't think you even noticed I was missing, you were so busy kissing ass—or don't you remember that? Second of all, you can't cockblock my future opportunities. Part of respecting me, which you claim you do, means understanding that my life will go on after our little agreement is over. Once this year is up, I'm going to have a whole life of my own to go back to, and part of that life will probably include new opportunities that I'll want to pursue. Professionally *and* personally."

I was fuming. Was she not feeling any of the same things I was, then? And why did she have to keep bringing up next year? Constantly reminding me that this marriage had an expiration date, like our divorce couldn't come quickly enough for her.

Regardless of our marital status, I hated thinking that other men were flirting with her—and I hated even more that she seemed to be counting down the days until she could actually do something about it. Because I knew for a fact that Andrew Apellido had been making a pass at Emzee, even if she didn't realize the truth. I'd recognized that look in his eyes. I was a guy, and I knew how guys thought. I had probably intervened just in time.

Emzee was *mine*.

Even if she wasn't mine.

"Look, Em—"

"*No.* I'm done talking to you right now," she cut me off.

Then she scooped up Munchkin and stormed off to the guest room, leaving me angry and horny and confused. Why the hell did I feel this way? Why couldn't I just keep my mouth shut and let Em do her thing? Was I really so jealous over that dickbag from New York? Maybe our friends-with-benefits situation just wasn't doing it for me any longer.

Maybe I needed something more.

Emzee didn't come to bed that night. I lay there for a while, waiting, but finally accepted that she was staying in the other room. She'd been editing photos in there and ignoring me every time I poked my head in the door to attempt a conversation.

When I tried to sleep, I could only toss and turn.

Fuck this. I'm going to win her, I decided.

Regardless of what happened next, I wasn't going down without a fight. I was a Malone, and when a Malone wanted something, they sure as hell got it.

Emzee would see. I was going to become the only man she had eyes for, in any room. I'd make sure that when we were together, she would be on *my* arm, at *my* side. Scum like Andrew Apellido wouldn't even dare look at her while she was with me, and they certainly wouldn't try to steal her away with their shitty business cards and false promises of helping her career.

I was going to make Emzee mine. Now and for always.

No matter the cost.

EMZEE

CHAPTER 15

Days later, my anger at Ford had faded but still not completely dissipated.

Things between us were more or less civil, but there was a new distance that hadn't been there before. Gone were the cozy, shared breakfasts with classic jazz playing softly in the background, and though we still had our evening walks with Munchkin—as safe as the neighborhood was, Ford refused to let me go by myself—they were no longer a chance for us to laugh and catch up with each other while strolling with casually linked arms.

Admittedly, it was mostly my fault. I was blatantly avoiding my husband. Working as much as possible, leaving in the morning before he woke up and getting home far past dinner time, communicating with him only when necessary and using one-word responses, going to bed early in the guest room where I'd set up camp for the foreseeable future.

I had assumed today would be exactly the same agonizing routine all over again. But when I got home from a DRM photoshoot early enough to take Munchkin for a pre-sundown walk, I found that the apartment was in the middle of a reformation.

The first thing that hit me was the smell. It was almost like a chemical, or—

"Careful," Ford said, coming out of the bedroom with a leashed Munchkin in his arms. "I think the paint is still wet."

I walked into the living room, gaping at the walls, which had been repainted a beautiful, muted shade of cool, grayish blue—exactly as I had suggested. It contrasted beautifully with the warm leather of the sofa and lightened up the entire room. And then I looked over at the mantel and let out a gasp at what I saw.

"It's always been one of my favorites—I hope you like it hung up there," Ford said.

Hanging over the fireplace was a huge, blown-up copy of a photo that I had taken years ago on a spring break trip to Serbia, where the Zoric family originally emigrated from.

"Subotica, right?" Ford asked. "I thought it would be cool to have something Serbian around here to look at. So you can have your own stamp on things."

The city of Subotica was known for its swooping, fairy tale-esque architecture and soft pastel-colored buildings, city halls, and churches. I had adored the place even before stepping off the train with Emiko, one of my art school friends, and we had both taken tons of pictures—especially of the Raichle Palace, a gorgeous Art Nouveau confection of arched windows, lacy iron balconies, mosaic tiles, and peachy pink and cobalt façades. It had been converted into an art gallery, and I spent an entire day wandering around by myself in there. I was way more interested in snapping photos of the architecture than in paying attention to any of the art.

Afterward, I'd dragged my exhausted self to meet back up with Emiko at Boss Caffe. We got a table on the outdoor patio under a shady canopy of trees and gorged ourselves on steaks with gorgonzola sauce and a sampling of desserts—pistachio cake, baklava with pear sorbet, a decadent chocolate torte, and šomloi galuška. It had been a perfect, unforgettable day.

"Was it not a good choice?" Ford asked, startling me out of my memories. He sounded concerned. "I can put something else up if you want—"

"No, no. It's perfect," I murmured, still choked up. "I love it."

"Great. I made a few other changes, too," Ford said. "Come see."

He handed Munchkin to me and I followed him as he pointed out the now floral-less bathroom, the tossed-out gold pillows, the general removal of all things overtly Claudia.

As we turned the corner into the den, I braced myself for facetime with the painting I hated so much, but to my shock, it was gone.

"Where'd the Le Comte go?" I asked suspiciously, eyes darting around as if I expected the thing to jump out at me from behind a piece of furniture.

"I had it moved into storage. I thought we could find something new to go there," he said.

I stood there for a minute, tongue-tied. This was the last thing I had expected to come home to. "But—I thought you loved the way your apartment looked before," I sputtered.

"Nah," he said with a shrug. "I was never that into Claudia's style. Too flashy."

Well. That was confusing. Especially since, just a few weeks ago, he had fought so hard to keep everything the way it had been. I didn't understand. What the hell did it all mean? Was he finally getting over Claudia? Or had he simply argued with me before because he was stubborn and hated the idea of change? Which...if that was the case, why redecorate *now*?

I opened my mouth to ask Ford what had gotten into him, but then closed it again. I didn't want to question things too much—I was happy enough that the changes were happening. And that I wouldn't hate my surroundings anymore.

"You're welcome to add your own touch," he told me. "This is just a start. I know you like soothing colors and less...man stuff."

Although I wanted to jump right on that, I refrained.

"Honestly," I told him, "I really appreciate the changes, but I'm only here for a year, you know? This is really nice, though. Thank you."

Was it just my imagination, or did Ford seem to visibly deflate at the reminder of our expiration date? But no. Couldn't be. The one year time limit had always been *his* idea.

"No problem," he said, and whatever it was that I thought I'd seen in his eyes, it was now gone. Looking down at his fancy watch, he added, "You do need to hurry up and get changed—we have reservations."

"Umm, for what?" I asked, my anxiety kicking into high gear.

Had I forgotten about another of Ford's obligatory work events, or worse—a dinner with his parents?

"Dinner," Ford said. "I thought it would be nice to take you out on a date. That's what newlyweds do, right?"

"What kind of dinner?" I asked slyly, though behind my

teasing tone, I had a case of the warm fuzzies. Ford was taking me on a date—a real date.

"It's a surprise," he said. "Can we be out the door in thirty minutes or less?"

"Depends," I said. "Is it a fancy surprise? Or a jeans-and-T-shirt surprise?"

"Probably not jeans. But not so fancy that you need to wear a ball gown either."

I laughed. "This tells me nothing, and yes, I can swing it."

"Here." Ford held out his arms. "I'll take Munch for a walk while you get ready."

I practically swooned. *This* was the Ford Malone I'd crushed on for so many years.

While the boys were gone, I excitedly got ready. I scrunched a little product in my hair to give myself voluminous, beachy waves, touched up my eyeliner, powdered my nose, and then turned the glam up to eleven with my favorite (but rarely-called-for) red lipstick. Vavoom.

When it came to my dress, I wanted something appropriately date-worthy, so I slipped into a vintage cocktail dress I'd been saving for a special occasion. It had sheer fabric along the neckline, a short tiered skirt, and looked perfect with my siren red kitten heels.

I still had no idea what had gotten into Ford.

Maybe he'd realized how ridiculous he'd been about the Andrew Apellido thing. Or how much it sucked for me to be living in an apartment that was a shrine to his ex-girlfriend. No matter the reason, I was just grateful that things seemed to be changing. For the better.

The date was much sweeter than I expected. Ford took me to an upscale fondue restaurant where we started our evening dipping various breads and veggies into various bowls of melty, artisanal cheeses. Raclette, Emmenthaler, mascarpone, Gruyère—I was practically moaning with every bite. It was heavenly. Also fun and a little messy, and I couldn't stop giggling as Ford kept losing his forkfuls of food in the bubbling bowls of cheese.

We were also served a salad course and a round of delectable small plates including crispy brussels sprouts, potstickers, and Castelvetrano olives. It was all delicious and the restaurant itself was cozy and romantic, giving off almost an English library vibe with its candlelight and dark patterned wallpaper.

I was ready to burst by the time dessert came, but I couldn't say no to the melted chocolate fountain and the plump, red strawberries that accompanied it. And I especially couldn't say no when Ford dipped the largest berry in the chocolate and held it out for me to eat.

After dinner, we walked to a nearby gallery that Ford had chosen. It was a new venue, one I hadn't even heard about yet.

When we walked through the doors, I blurted out an, "Oh my God."

The images on the walls were by a photographer I loved —a lesser known Ghanaian artist who hadn't gotten the acclaim I was certain they deserved. I had both of their photography books but had never seen their work in person.

"How did you know?" I asked Ford.

After all, he had planned the whole evening. There was no way this was a coincidence.

"I pay attention," he said with a pleased smirk.

I had no idea what had come over him, why this night felt so different, but damn, I liked it. The whole date felt like something out of a dream.

We wandered around the gallery for over an hour. Ford

was tuned in to the eclectic variety of artists on display but still completely attentive to me, asking questions about what I saw in a particular photograph or what I thought about the abstract mixed media sculptures. He was interested in both the art and my opinions, and with each passing minute, I found myself wanting him more and more. When he casually took my hand in his, brushing his fingers softly along my knuckles, I became even more wet for him. And I wasn't wearing any underwear, which only served to turn me on even more.

Reaching the last room in the gallery, I started to move back the way we had come, but Ford stopped me.

"This way," he said, leading me out a door in the far wall.

I thought we were simply going home, but instead, Ford nodded his head at a roof access staircase along the side of the building. He started his upward ascent and I followed, feeling the evening breeze tickling the bare skin of my legs, the swirl of cool air moving upward, another reminder of my lack of undergarments. My need for Ford tugged at my lower belly, making my knees weaken on the climb.

Once we got up on the roof, I was delighted at the view of the city. All the buildings felt so close, like I could almost reach out and touch the glitter and glass, the golden light spilling from the windows. It was incredible. Chicago's angular urban beauty spread out all around us, a blanket of stars overhead, the rooftop bathed in the glow of neon.

"It's beautiful," I breathed.

"You're beautiful," Ford said, coming from behind to wrap his arms around me.

Even though his body was warm against mine, I shivered.

Turning in his arms, I tilted my face up to meet his kiss.

It was harsh, demanding, and urgent. Apparently I hadn't been the only one thinking naughty thoughts during our gallery tour.

I slid my hand down his chest, his abs, down the front of his pants, where I could feel how much he wanted me. When I wrapped my hand around his cock, he moaned in my mouth.

Still kissing me, his hands slipped under the hem of my dress, stroking the soft skin of my inner thighs. When he reached my pussy, soaked and aching for him, I felt his body go still.

He lifted his head, his eyes brimming with lust.

"No panties tonight?"

I shook my head. He pushed a finger inside me and I let out a whimper.

"You're wet," he said.

"I've been wet all night," I told him, grabbing his hand to steady it as I started to slowly ride his finger, keeping my eyes on his the whole time.

"That's so fucking sexy," he groaned, sliding another finger inside me.

"Yes," I gasped, my head falling back. I widened my legs and leaned against the brick half-wall as Ford began to fuck me with his fingers, his lips hot on my neck, his teeth teasing and nipping at me. "More," I moaned, my fingers digging into his biceps as I bucked on his hand.Without hesitating, Ford turned me around so I could grab the lip of the brick wall, and I did, staring out at the gorgeous view of the city at night. He tugged the skirt of my dress up, exposing my ass to the cool air, and then I heard the rasp of his zipper being undone.

"Fuck me, Ford—"

But before I could get any more dirty talk out, he was

inside me, pumping hard and fast, like he couldn't wait even one more second to fuck me.

I cried out, my moans lost on the wind as Ford fucked me against the wall. Both of us were gasping for breath, and he was whispering my name, squeezing my tits through my dress with one rough hand and slapping my ass with the other. I felt like a goddess. Knowing we could get caught at any moment only made me hotter. Wetter. Louder.

There was no buildup, no crest. Out of nowhere I just shattered, coming so hard and deep I was shaking all over with the force of my orgasm. With his hand clutching my ass, Ford let out a groan and finished at the same time, cursing as he spilled into me. We stayed there, gazing out at the city, letting our hearts slow, until Ford carefully pulled out and turned me around.

"Mrs. Malone," he said formally, tugging my skirt back down. "Shall we head home?"

I nodded, and he arranged his jacket over my shoulders before taking my hand.

As we made our way back to the car, I realized that I didn't know what was happening between us. All I knew was that it felt dangerous.

I was going to end up with a broken heart.

EMZEE

CHAPTER 16

Yet another dinner with Ford's parents was getting ready to start.

Oh, joy.

If I could have come up with a good enough excuse to get out of it, I would have, but the bigger problem was that these Malone family dinners were something that Ford did on a regular basis—there was no way I could avoid them forever. So it was time to face the music.

I just needed to figure out how to coexist with the Malones peacefully. Or at least, coexist with them peacefully for the duration of a meal. How hard could it be?

At least for round two, I had a better idea of what to expect...and what was expected of me as the hostess. Thus I'd gone into this enterprise tonight with a careful eye toward doing things more like the Malones wanted. Not exactly like they'd been done in the past, but a compromise that I hoped we all could live with.

No creative tablescapes, no exotic takeout food. They wanted china dishes and a personal chef? Fine. I'd give it to them. The best wine, chosen by a sommelier. The best menu, put together by a professional. The best everything. Eat your heart out, snobs.

Despite myself, I had to admit that I felt a bit of grudging respect for Claudia. No matter what I thought of her, she'd put up with these family dinners for years and somehow managed to hold on to her sanity through all of it.

I knew Mrs. Malone (and to a lesser extent, her husband) would never accept me the way they'd accepted Claudia, that no matter how nice dinner was, they'd still never allow me to stay married to Ford. But I was going to try to please them anyway. I didn't really have a choice.

And I swore to myself that I wouldn't let their comments get under my skin again. I would be prepared for whatever insults they threw at me. I'd stay strong. Not that a drink wouldn't help, which was why I had all the martini fixings ready to go. Ford had said his parents liked them, and I knew I'd need more than wine to fortify me for the long evening ahead.

The doorbell rang, and I straightened my cardigan, put Munchkin in his kennel, and headed for the door. Ford had his hand on the knob as I came up behind him.

"Here goes nothing," I murmured.

"You'll be fine," Ford said, as if he'd somehow forgotten what a complete disaster our last family dinner night had been.

"There's my boy!" Mrs. Malone screeched the second she walked in. "And...Mara."

"Hello," I managed to say politely as she smothered Ford in a hug and an accompanying perfume cloud. As Ford helped her out of her coat, I turned to Ford's dad. "And how are you, Mr. Malone?"

"I've been better," he answered noncommittally.

"I saw that the Dow closed at three points up today," I

said, grateful I'd checked the stock market report earlier so I'd have something to say to him. "So there's some good news."

Mr. Malone's face immediately brightened. "Yes, I suppose that's true."

"Shall we?" Ford said, gesturing toward the dining room.

As we shuffled along, I leaned closer to Ford's dad and whispered, "There's more good news. I may have arranged a double helping of dessert for you as well."

They say the way to a man's heart is through his stomach, but it hadn't escaped me that Mr. Malone had devoured his coconut sorbet after our last dinner—as well as my portion—so I'd taken a gamble and decided to feed his sweet tooth this time. Judging by his bright eyes, the gamble had paid off. I may have secured myself a Malone ally after all.

I made cocktails for the Malones once they were seated at the table. A very dry martini with two pimento stuffed olives for Father Malone, and a dirty martini with a plain olive for Mother Malone. Ford had coached me in advance on how to prepare the drinks, but I couldn't tell if I'd impressed the Malones judging by their post-sip faces. But hey, at least neither of them had spit their drink across the room.

Meanwhile, Ford made gin and tonics for the two of us, and when the chef popped his head into the dining room to tell us the food was ready, the heavenly smells coming from the kitchen hit us full force.

"Mmm," I sighed.

"And what, precisely, are we having?" Mrs. Malone asked, brow raised.

"French," I said. I wasn't being coy, exactly—I just

couldn't even begin to pronounce half the dishes we were about to be served. I wasn't worried, though.

Pierre was the most highly awarded chef in the greater Chicago area, and I'd been lucky to book him for a four-person meal when he was accustomed to larger private parties and events for the very wealthy. Luckily, the Malone family name carried a lot of weight around town. Once I'd explained who the dinner was for, Pierre had been more than happy to cater.

"We love French," Mr. Malone said, still looking perky and obviously attempting to be diplomatic. "Don't we, dear?"

Mrs. Malone ignored him, turning instead to Ford. "You look tired," she said. "Long day?" Then she cut her eyes at me, as if Ford's exhaustion was clearly my fault alone.

"Uh, I feel fine, actually," Ford said, taking a healthy swig of his gin.

In my humble opinion, he looked *damn* fine. He was wearing a charcoal shirt and matching pants, his sleeves rolled up just enough to show off his drool-worthy forearms. As for me, under my pale pink cardigan (a shade purchased specifically to please Mrs. Malone), I had on a modest black dress and flats. I thought we made a rather decent-looking pair.

"I'm a bit tired myself," Mr. Malone said.

"I didn't ask you," Mrs. Malone told her husband with a scowl.

Before they could devolve into full-blown bickering, we were rescued by Pierre's assistant, Jacques, who was bringing out the first course.

I'd specified that the meal be served on the infamous china that Ford and Claudia had bought, but this time we weren't having steak. We were having the best French food in Chicago. Take that, Claudia.

"Bon appétit," Jacques said with a flourish, ducking back into the kitchen.

We started with the most delicate escargot I'd ever had, the snails perfectly cooked in butter and herbs. I'd never cared much for them, to be honest, but they practically melted in my mouth. I sopped up the rest of the dipping sauce with a fresh, crusty slice of hot bread.

The next course was a petite salad garnished with watermelon radishes, followed by mussels marinières steamed in a lemony broth made with leeks, shallots, and garlic.

"These mussels are fantastic," Mr. Malone said dreamily. "Straight from the market this morning, I'd wager."

"That's exactly right," I said. "I told Pierre to prepare whatever he picked up fresh today, and I'd say he hasn't disappointed."

While the ingredients were insanely expensive enough for Ford's dad to appreciate, the portions seemed tiny and fancy enough for Mrs. Malone to enjoy, even if she wouldn't admit it.

The main course was confit de canard. The duck was meltingly tender, the skin golden and crisp. It was served over a pile of buttery fried new potatoes and fresh greens fanned out along the edge of the plate. Everybody dug in, too busy eating to keep up with the small talk.

The Malones hadn't complimented me once during the meal, but they hadn't insulted me either, and frankly, that was a win. As far as I was concerned, Pierre was worth every penny.

It wasn't until dessert was brought out that the conversation started back up. Over bittersweet chocolate soufflé, I started to notice something—despite all of Mama Malone's fawning, Ford's parents actually seemed to criticize him just as much as they had criticized me at the last dinner. As if they didn't think *he* was good enough either.

And without my tablescape or menu to fuss over, they were going at him full force.

"Your father has some thoughts about your latest deal," Mrs. Malone said.

"What's the issue? The deal was fine," Ford said, looking to his dad.

"Now, now, what I said was that—" Mr. Malone started.

"It was disappointing," Ford's mother interrupted. "You could have gotten at least another quarter million if you had just pushed harder."

"They would've walked," Ford said. "They were skittish to begin with."

"No one walks away from Malone Real Estate Holdings," his mother said. "They would have caved. They always do. And we really need to discuss your latest hire."

She wasn't eating her soufflé at all, but she was on her fourth martini.

"My latest hire is also fine," Ford said.

"That's the problem," Ford's mother said. "You seem to think 'fine' is good enough. It's not. You have a family reputation to uphold. Your actions affect all of us."

Ford didn't say anything, but I noticed that he was getting less and less responsive with every criticism his mother heaped on top of him.

She didn't seem to notice. "And that new headshot of yours. We'll have to get that retaken. It's not appropriate. I mean honestly Ford, facial hair? It just isn't professional."

She waited for Ford to respond, but he didn't.

"Actually, people don't really mind a bit of scruff these

days," I cut in, unable to listen to her anymore. "The current generation is...less judgmental."

Mr. Malone nodded at me, though he didn't contradict his wife.

Still, I knew what I was talking about when it came to headshots, and Ford's mother was just plain wrong about Ford's. It was professional and well-lit and fit in well with every other photo that Malone Real Estate had on their site. If anything, the headshot of Ford's mother was the one that needed to be replaced. It was straight out of the eighties, with soft focus lighting and obvious Photoshopping that was clearly intended to make her look younger, but instead just made her skin look waxy and dull, like a doll's.

"The photo is good," I reiterated. "In my professional photographer's opinion."

Mrs. Malone just sniffed. Ford looked miserable. It made me want to stick up for him, so I figured I might as well sing his praises.

"I'm not sure if Ford mentioned it," I said, "but he gave a seminar on the business of real estate last weekend for my nonprofit, and the students absolutely loved it. He's an excellent teacher. And if he's half as good at his job as he is at talking about it, I have complete faith that he's worth his weight in gold at MREH."

Ford's parents were both staring at me now. Then a smile—one I didn't trust—forced its way onto Mrs. Malone's face.

"Well isn't that *lovely*," she cooed. "I've heard all about your little charity, Mara. All the good it does. And you know what, we should all be helping out. Don't you think so, Ford?"

"Ford already helped out a lot by teaching the class," I tried to say, but his mother ignored me.

"I think we should throw a big fundraiser to help out, don't you?" she kept going. "A big shindig, with all of Chicago's cream of the crop. Why, I know the *perfect* person to help."

My heart sank. I knew exactly who she meant and where all of this was going. And the worst part was, I'd basically walked right on into it.

Ford's parents were taking over, just like they'd done with my marriage. Only this time, they had their sights set on my charity—inserting fucking Claudia into the one thing in my life that I was most proud of, which frankly I'd busted my ass to build from the ground up.

Claudia. It was always Claudia.

I couldn't help wondering if there was some sort of blackmail at play. Did Claudia's family somehow own the Malones, have dirt on them the way the Malones had something on my family? It would make sense.

I looked over at Ford, hoping he would object. But as usual, he didn't.

Instead he just looked at me and shrugged. "Claudia *is* good at fundraisers."

My heart sank even lower.

"You see?" Mrs. Malone crowed. "It will be perfect."

Right. Of course it would be.

EMZEE

CHAPTER 17

I managed to keep my composure about the Claudia/fundraiser situation while Ford's parents were still over, for Ford's sake. The last thing I wanted to do was stand up for him one moment and then go on the attack the next over him not defending me. But I couldn't wait for the senior Malones to depart, so Ford and I could be alone again. Because I was ready to unload.

As soon as we'd all said our good nights and Jacques and Pierre had left, I turned on Ford.

"I think that went...slightly better than last time," he said. "All things considered."

"Why did you let your parents say that Claudia could help with the program?" I blurted.

He looked at me blankly.

"I...thought it was a good idea," he said. "Don't you want the program to get more exposure? That's what Claudia's good at. Her family is even better connected than mine. She knows everybody."

"But it's *Claudia*! Are you seriously going to stand here and tell me you think she has my best interests in mind?"

Of course I liked the idea of promoting the program, getting more support and attention focused on it. And we could definitely benefit from more donations—and ideally more mentors. But at the same time, I was concerned about what Claudia would do with something I cared about so much in her vengeful, perfectly manicured hands. She knew how important See Yourself was to me. I didn't trust her one bit, and I really didn't want her involved.

Ford frowned, as if the implications of having his ex-girlfriend throw a fundraiser for someone she despised were only just now starting to sink in.

"Shit," he said. "I didn't even think—"

"No. You didn't. That's the problem."

Stalking down the hall to the bedroom, I tried to slow my breathing. I knew my anger was clouding my judgment. The thing was, it felt like we had *just* gotten Claudia's ghost out of the apartment, out of our lives, and now she'd been invited right back in—and onto my turf, no less. See Yourself was the one area of my life where I should have had full control. But as far as the Malones were concerned, nothing, not even the nonprofit I had founded, was sacred. The power was all theirs.

"Em," Ford said gently, following me into the room.

I let Munchkin out of his kennel, where he'd been forlornly awaiting his liberation all evening, and he shot straight to Ford without so much as a thank-you slobber for me first.

"Traitor," I murmured, shaking my head. To Ford, I said, "I'm getting ready for bed."

When I slid under the covers beside him twenty minutes and one hot shower later, I was slightly more calm. Before I could say anything, Ford had turned to me and taken my hand.

I'm sorry," he told me. "I was just so focused on what a great opportunity it would be for you and the program that I wasn't even thinking about Claudia. I understand if you want to call the whole thing off."

Sighing, I shook my head. "I don't know. I feel like the ball is already rolling. It just makes me so anxious to have my nemesis in charge of anything to do with the nonprofit."

Ford nodded, his eyes searching mine. "I understand. Although at this point, she honestly seems to mean more to you than she does to me."

For a second, I couldn't process his words. Was he trying to say that Claudia didn't matter to him anymore? That I cared more about their former relationship than he did?

"I meant what I said before," he went on. "I can get rid of Claudia if you want."

"Okay..." I said, waiting for the other shoe to drop.

"But before I do, maybe you can really think about everything you could accomplish with her and my parents' backing. I know it sounds shitty, but we should take advantage of it. You and your mentees would have access to so many resources. Isn't that the most important thing?"

"I will think about it," I said, leaning back against my pillows.

Ford turned off the lights, and we settled in, but I couldn't get comfortable, and I wasn't even remotely tired with the way my brain was kicking into overdrive.

Ugh. I hated to admit it, but Ford was right. I was being unreasonable.

I couldn't let my feelings for Claudia get in the way of something that could be genuinely beneficial to my organization in the long run. Because as much as I disliked her on a personal level, I also knew that she was a pro when it came to hosting fundraisers and galas. It was practically her superpower.

Sure, she'd probably use any opportunity she could to get back in with Ford, but she was probably going to do that anyway, fundraising or not. After all, she had the rest of the Malone family on her side. I should probably be grateful that she hadn't been invited to dinner tonight.

The other (depressingly obvious) thing I needed to take into account was that my relationship with Ford wasn't even real. Our whole marriage was a sham—a sham with a ticking clock attached to it. I had no right to be jealous and possessive about his exes. Especially since there was no doubt in my mind that the minute the ink had dried on the divorce papers, Claudia would be all over him, offering him her "support." It was inevitable.

Even though I hated thinking about it, I had to be realistic.

Did I want to work with Claudia? Hells to the no. Did I know—in my deepest of hearts—that she would be able to bring money and attention to a cause I would give my right tit for? Yes. There were just so many people we could help with this.

Mid-turmoil, Munchkin let out a cartoonishly loud doggie snore from his bed across the room. Ford let out a chuckle, and then Munchie did it again, and before I knew it I was joining in with the giggles, Ford and I both laughing until we were gasping for breath.

"He sounds like the tiniest little chainsaw," I said, which set off Ford all over again.

Once I had myself under control, I slid over to Ford's side of the bed and climbed on top of him, nuzzling his neck as his hands came around to massage my back.

"Okay," I said, sighing.

Ford paused. "Okay what?"

Judging by the growing bulge in his pants, he had no idea that I was referring to the fundraiser, rather than suggesting we have sex. Not that I was opposed.

"I'll let the fundraiser happen. I'll accept Claudia's help," I said. "Your parents' too. If they're willing to help with See Yourself, I'd be happy to have them."

He took a moment before saying, "I'm glad. I think it's the right thing to do."

I wasn't exactly sure about that myself, but I hoped he was right. While we were on the topic of his parents, however, there was one more thing I wanted to discuss.

"One more thing," I said, just as Ford slid his hand down the back of my pj pants.

His hand stilled, mid-grab. "Yes?" he asked.

It was clear from his tone that he was done talking. But this was important.

"I don't understand your relationship with your parents," I said. "Why you're so set on pleasing them all the time when it seems like nothing you do ever makes them happy."

"That's not true," Ford said defensively.

"It isn't? They were nothing but disparaging tonight," I pointed out. "Your mom found something to criticize about everything—the deal you made, your new hire, even your headshot. And your dad, no offense, might be the most passive person I've ever met."

Ford sighed, kissed my forehead, and then gently moved my body off of his. Apparently any possibility of sex was now off the table.

"My parents have high standards," he said. "All Malones do."

Then he rolled over, his back facing me.

"Why do you let them be so hard on you?" I asked, refusing to let it go so easily.

"I don't *let* them do anything."

"But—"

"You don't know anything about my family," he said harshly. "Let it go."

"Well, I'd like to," I said. "I'd like to understand."

I held my breath, hoping he would talk to me. Confide in me. Like he used to back in high school. And for a long, long moment, I thought he might. But then he just let out a sigh.

"It's complicated," he said. "End of discussion."

Feeling dejected, I stared up at the ceiling, listening to his breathing smooth out, wondering if I'd ever get the truth about his family. If I'd ever get the truth about *anything* from him.

Maybe it was time to stop hoping I would.

EMZEE

CHAPTER 18

The last time I'd been called in for a private conference at DRM with my brothers, Stefan had told us that the Russian mob was threatening our family. I was praying today's team meeting wouldn't be a repeat of that. I'd gotten more than enough negativity dumped on me lately.

"Sorry I'm late!" I apologized as I burst through the door. "It took forever to get Munch checked in at the doggie daycare, and then the traffic downtown was—"

"It's all good," Luka said. "Have a seat."

Neither he nor Stefan looked as if the executioner's axe was about to drop, so I relaxed a little into my chair as Stefan poured us all coffee. And I took it as a good sign that my brothers seemed unbothered by my tardiness. Maybe they even had some positive news to share.

How wrong I was.

"Things going okay at home?" Stefan asked me. "You and Ford getting along?"

"Um." My cheeks heated, and I took a quick gulp of coffee to stall. "We're great," I lied.

"Good, good," Stefan said, nodding. "What about See Yourself? Still going strong?"

I glanced over at Luka, confused about the line of questioning, but he wouldn't meet my gaze. "The nonprofit is fine. Ford just taught a fantastic real estate seminar and the Malones are helping put together a big fundraiser for it. I'm not sure when, but you'll all be invited."

"Nice," Luka said, forcing a smile. "I can't wait."

Enough was enough.

"Why are you two acting so weird?" I huffed, looking back and forth between my brothers. "And what's with the interrogation? I thought we were here to talk about Danica Rose, not my personal life. Somebody better start talking."

Luka rubbed his eyes and let out a sigh. "All right, Stefan," he said. "Why don't you get down to it?"

Instinctively, I held my breath. Of course it would have been too much to hope that the Russian mob would just disappear on its own. But that was exactly why I'd bargained with the devil—er, Mrs. Malone. In order to make the Bratva go away. Was she not holding up her end of the agreement? My stomach started to churn.

Stefan nodded. "Okay. The reason I'm asking about your life is because...there's still a very real possibility looming that DRM will go under and all of us will end up jobless and starting from scratch—"

"If not actually murdered in our sleep," Luka cut in.

"Luka!" Stefan scolded.

"Sorry," Luka said with a shrug. "I'm just saying."

"Anyway. I'm still not convinced we'll be able to work things out with the Bratva, so I'd like all of us to have a contingency plan in place. The subject certainly bears consideration," Stefan finished.

"Hope for the best and prepare for the worst?" I added.

My brothers nodded grimly.

"I can appreciate the practicality," I said, trying to lighten the mood.

"Yeah," Luka said drily. "Thanks for that, Dad."

"Look, at the end of the day I'm not trying to run anyone's life—I just want to make sure we're all okay." Stefan looked grim as he drank his coffee.

"What will you do if the agency folds?" I asked him.

I felt a little sick just saying it out loud. I didn't miss what KZ Modeling had been, but Danica Rose was *ours*. My brothers and I had built the agency back up from the charred ashes of personal and professional ruin that our criminal father had left it in, and it would break my heart if it was taken away from us. Especially because of something our father had done.

"I've been thinking about it," Stefan confessed, leaning back in his chair. "Especially with a baby on the way. But I'll be fine. I've made a ton of business connections and I know I could hit up my contacts and find someone looking for help running their company."

Smiling, I added, "And with Tori's Linguistics degree and her gift for languages, international business would be a natural next step if it comes down to it."

"Indeed," Stefan said. He looked over at Luka, who nodded.

"Brooklyn and I will be okay too," Luka said. "I'm sure if we put feelers out, we'd find clients interested in any kind of advertising and marketing firm we started. And actually, with Brooklyn's background in modeling and my MBA, we could encapsulate whatever type of modeling business we want, and use her experience and connections to get it off the ground."

Now both of my brothers were looking at me expectantly, and I realized that this meeting was more about *my* plans than theirs. They seemed to have everything well in hand, but they were obviously worried about what would happen to their little sister if DRM folded.

I was both touched and annoyed at their concern. After all, I was an adult, too. A grown-ass woman with a fancy photography degree, a banging portfolio under my belt, and —most importantly—years of professional job experience

"Guess I'll find out if art really *can* pay the bills," I said lightly.

They exchanged a look.

"What about Ford?" Stefan asked. "You think he'd be okay with supporting you for a bit, if necessary? Just until you figure things out."

Bristling at the insinuation that I might not be able to pull my own weight with my photography gigs, I lashed out with, "Well he can certainly afford to cover me, can't he?"

I was feeling more snappish than they'd probably expected, even though it wasn't their fault that we were in this mess—and it really wasn't their fault that I'd entered into a contract first with Ford and then with his family... both of which were bound to make me miserable at the end of the year. But I still wasn't ready to admit any of that to my brothers.

They had no idea I'd gambled all of our futures—and the future of Danica Rose—on my fake marriage, hoping against hope that the upcoming year would give us enough time to pull off this *deus ex machina*.

I decided I'd better head them off at the pass before they could ask more questions about me and Ford, so I volunteered, "I was actually just speaking with Andrew Apellido about a job opportunity recently. Have you heard of him?"

"Andrew Apellido?" Luka's eyebrows went up. "Holy

shit, dude's a legend! I love that guy. He launched a new magazine project a few months ago. Stefan, have you checked it out?"

"I am now," Stefan said, tapping at his smartphone screen.

"Brooklyn was on the cover for their third issue, and the photos were *insanely* cool. Right up your alley type of stuff, Em," Luka said. "How'd you meet him?"

"At a party," I said. "He knows all about Danica Rose and he's familiar with my work."

Both of my brothers looked impressed.

"Okay, now I remember," Stefan said, still scrolling away at his screen. "They ran this great long-form piece about the influence of Eastern Europe on Western media." He looked up at me, head cocked. "Shame you're already married. Someone like Andrew could really bring a lot to the table."

"Way to be mercenary," Luka joked. "Emzee married for love, remember?"

I laughed along with them, but Stefan had no idea how close to my own thoughts his words had been. Because ever since my fortuitous introduction to Andrew, I'd been feeling more aware than ever that I *did* have a life of my own to pursue. Especially once I was divorced.

Just like I had told Ford in the heat of the moment, the world wasn't going to end when my relationship did. It might feel that way to me, but time always healed. And even though my mourning wouldn't be an act, there would always be another act to follow. I'd get through it.

"Oh, Em, were you planning on going to the Borderless Business Convention next week?" Stefan asked. "Luka's coming with me, but if you want I can book you on our flight."

"Where is it? I remember hearing about it, but not the details."

"New York," Stefan said. "I'm hoping to convince the Weston brothers to buy out a portion of our company. Not a controlling interest or anything, but..."

"We could obviously use the cash," Luka said.

Right. To pay off the Bratva. Because my deal with the Malones was a secret. I wished I could tell them about it, but part of me was still afraid it might fall through. The Malones could renege at any moment. The other thing was, the less my brothers knew about my deal, the better. I knew they'd only try to talk me out of it, maybe even approach the Malones themselves—if I could just pull this off on my own, my family and DRM would be saved. I'd tell them about all of it afterward, when there'd be no chance of them screwing things up, best of intentions or not.

I gave them a smile. "I'll sit this one out, but thanks. I've got enough on my plate at the moment. Good luck, though. I really hope you make some headway with them. Fingers crossed."

My answer was cheery and chirpy—just as they'd expect from their little sister.

Back in my own office, I closed the door and let out a breath of relief.

As full of warm fuzzies as I was over my brothers' care and concern for me, it was so much work pretending. I hated doing it, hated the constant lying, but it couldn't be helped. We all had secrets. Unfortunately, mine felt like they were threatening to overwhelm me.

I just had to get through the next year and hope that if I couldn't pull off the deal with the Malones, maybe Stefan could work something out with the Weston brothers. If he could, good God, it would solve a lot of my problems. Both for the Zoric family and for me personally. I sent up a little prayer that the meeting would go well, that it might give us some options.

Because as it stood right now, *everything* was riding on my divorce.

A divorce I wasn't even sure I wanted.

EMZEE

CHAPTER 19

"The Grand Ballroom here is absolutely *perfect* for what we have in mind," Claudia was saying to Ford, batting her eyes tartily.

I followed along behind them, wishing I hadn't agreed to this. As much as having Claudia plan a fundraiser for See Yourself was going to be good for the charity and my mentees, it didn't make me happy to be spending all this time with my husband's ex. Especially when she made it so clear that she didn't think much of our wedding vows.

Claudia had shown up for our first meeting this morning in a sleek jade green suit and Saint Laurent heels, hair blown out and makeup tastefully on point. As for me, I'd thrown on dark skinny jeans, my black eyeliner, and a tweed blazer with a swiss dot blouse underneath. It was hard not to feel like a hobo standing next to her. There was no comparison between us.

Where I was short and dark and curvy, Claudia was tall and blonde and thin. Her lipstick didn't even smudge when she drank the grapefruit Perrier the Four Seasons hotel staff had offered her on a silver tray upon our arrival.

And damn if I wasn't already missing the soothing emotions I'd experienced with my brothers during our family meeting at DRM. I could practically feel the cortisol pumping into my system with every *clip-clop* of Claudia's designer heels.

This was our third stop so far, after touring event spaces at the Shedd Aquarium and the Mid-America Club. We still had appointments at a few more of the richy-rich hotels in town, including the Waldorf and the Langham, but I was already daydreaming about begging off with an imaginary migraine. I'd much rather be home, binging *Outlander* on the couch with Munch.

Unfortunately, I trusted Claudia with my husband about as far as I could throw her.

Not only did she look good enough to eat, but she had the charm turned up to eleven today. And the Malones hadn't been bluffing, either—Claudia had an in at all the hottest spots in town. No matter where we went or who we spoke with, she was adored by everyone. I'd seen enough of those French double cheek kisses today to last me a lifetime.

As much as it pained me to admit it, she obviously knew these venues like the back of her perfectly mani-cured hand—and she had all the connections I lacked. I wouldn't accomplish half the things we were planning to do without her help. But I might have been able to appre-ciate those things a little more if she didn't take advantage of every possible opportunity to pretend I wasn't even there.

"The room is seventy-seven hundred square feet, and can accommodate up to five-hundred-sixty banquet guests," the hotel manager was telling us as he flung open the Grand Ballroom doors.

"You see what I was saying?" Claudia beamed, dragging

Ford up the staircase with her. "Isn't it terribly dramatic? And this is the coat check, the parlor suite..."

I followed along behind them, huffing to keep up.

As I lifted my camera to snap a few photos, I felt more like Claudia's assistant than the person for whom she was planning the fundraiser. Even the hotel manager was ignoring me, directing his speech about the state room's capacity at Claudia and Ford. It didn't help that my husband, in one of his bespoke suits, looked like he belonged with her.

And Claudia was doing her best to take advantage of that assumption.

I was just taking a few more pictures of the stunning chandelier overhead when Claudia said my name. I didn't immediately respond, so she snapped her fingers at me. Like I was a dog.

"Excuse you?" I said, my head whipping up. "Did you seriously just—"

"The ballroom is this way," Claudia told me, faux-sweetly. "Come along."

As she flounced ahead, I expected Ford to say something, but he was looking at his phone and didn't even seem to notice the casual disrespect that his ex had just flung my way. Meanwhile I was fuming so hard there was practically steam coming out of my ears.

"Ford," I hissed, but he was already halfway across the lobby, following the manager.

"I've put together dozens of incredibly successful events here," Claudia was bragging when I caught up with them. "What do you think?"

I couldn't help glaring daggers at her as she held out her arms and executed a twirl in the center of the polished parquet floor.

"Gorgeous," Ford said, nodding.

I kept reminding myself that I was doing this for the girls, but with every passing moment it became harder and harder to resist tripping Claudia in her heels so she'd fall flat on her face.

"We'd go for something classy and elegant, not necessarily a theme," Claudia was telling the hotel manager. Then she turned to Ford with a smirk. "Remember those tacky fundraisers we went to in college?"

Ford laughed. "How could I forget?"

Claudia continued, "Remember that horrible one at the marina our senior year? Half the guests got seasick and the other half got sick watching everyone else be seasick."

My husband was in stitches now. I had no idea Claudia was such a gifted comedienne.

"Oh yeah, that was disgusting," Ford said. Hardy har har.

"I don't think the school raised any money at all!" Claudia giggled. "That was the last time they let anyone from Gamma Kappa Omega plan one of their events. They should have known better, though, those girls were always such a disaster."

She gave me a pointed look. Even though I'd never been in a sorority, it was clear that she thought I would have fit right in with the "disaster girls."

"Luckily, this is a ballroom and not a boat," I pointed out dryly. Claudia ignored me. Then, inspiration struck. "Wait, what if we used part of the room as a gallery for some of my mentees' photography? We could even do a silent auction for the photos, get them framed..."

"That's an interesting idea," Ford said, nodding.

"It's very cute," Claudia cut in. "But this is a banquet, not show and tell for all your little art projects. Ford, I was actually thinking we should do something more like what I did for the polo team fundraiser."

Cute? Art projects? I stalked over, absolutely livid, but Claudia didn't even seem to notice. She just talked over me. Literally. I was about a head shorter than both of them.

"Remember that night, Ford?" Claudia was asking. "With the polo team?"

She stepped closer to him, wrapping a hand around his bicep. I held back a growl and firmly grabbed his other arm, flashing my wedding rings in Claudia's face.

"You know what night *I* remember, Ford?" I said, impersonating Claudia to a T.

"Why don't I show you and your husband the staging area," the manager said, cutting in.

With a sinking in my gut, I realized he was talking to *Claudia*.

"*My husband and I* would love to see the staging area," I said, making sure my voice was loud and clear.

Everyone looked at me, slightly startled.

"Oh," the manager said, looking uncomfortable. "I'm sorry, I thought—"

I waved off the apology. "Staging, please?"

Claudia had dropped her hand from Ford's arm, but her expression was stormy. As we all followed the manager, she came up alongside me. "That was unbearably rude," she said.

"I agree," I said. I was just about to tell her exactly how rude when Ford joined us.

"What was that all about?" he asked me.

Claudia frowned. "I'm not sure Emzee wants my help," she said. "And if I'm not wanted, well, I'm happy to just go and leave you to it."

Part of me wanted to tell her not to let the door hit her

in the ass on her way out, but I knew that if I wanted this fundraiser to be a success, I needed her.

"Don't go," Ford said. "I'm sure Em was just eager to see everything."

"Yep," I said, grinding my back teeth together. "That's what it was."

Claudia gave Ford a dazzling smile. "I'm so glad we're working together," she told him. "We always made such a good team, don't you think?"

My nails were digging into my palms.

"I guess we did," Ford said.

"Remember that time in Ibiza?" Claudia asked. "We had so much fun traveling. All those adventures."

Ford chuckled and patted Claudia's arm. "That was a long time ago. Another life."

"I think we should focus on the fundraiser," I said, hoping to remind both of them that I was literally standing right there. "We still have a ton of logistics to iron out."

Claudia glanced over at me and waved a hand dismissively. "I've been doing this for a long time. Once we pick a location, the rest will fall into place."

"I'm sure it's not that simple," I argued.

She gave me a look. "It's exactly that simple with me," she said with a condescending little laugh. "It's almost like you've never planned a fundraiser before."

There was a long pause and then another laugh.

"Oh, wait," she said, literally looking down her nose at me. "I guess you haven't."

She was right, dammit. I'd never planned a fundraiser before, and certainly not one of this scale.

"All I care about is raising money for See Yourself," I said, yet again feeling like a third wheel for my very own project. "I'm sure you'll do a great job."

Claudia did that condescending laugh again. "Well, of course, I will," she said. "It's not rocket science but it does take a particular kind of gentle touch."

She turned to Ford.

"And you know exactly how gentle my touch is, don't you, Ford?"

They both laughed, and I forced myself not to scream. Claudia obviously had Ford wrapped around her finger, because he had yet to speak up for me even once—or even seem to notice what was going on.

How dare that...Trust Fund Barbie keep putting the moves on my man. Even after I'd flashed my rings in her face! Our marriage might be fake, but Claudia didn't know that.

Or *did* she?

Because come to think of it, Ford seemed to be leaning into Claudia's flirtations, enjoying their little reunion way too much. Did he really not notice how manipulative his ex was being, how she was practically draping herself all over him, or was he simply not over her like I had thought he was? Or was this all some ploy to make me jealous?

Well. If it was, it was working—but I'd never admit to Ford that I was indeed jealous of Claudia. And I could certainly be outwardly pissed about the optics.

I'd just have to give him as much of a cold shoulder as he was giving me.

Which meant, unfortunately, that I was stuck listening to the two of them reminisce about the glory days of their past while I tried to focus on choosing a venue and ignoring them.

The rest of our tours for the day dragged on similarly (if not worse), with me trailing along behind Claudia and Ford and not even trying to engage.

Ultimately, over a painfully unhurried dinner at Shanghai Terrace (Claudia was a member of the Peninsula Hotel's exclusive Supper Club, of course, so she secured us a table on the spot—and then ordered for all of us in obnoxiously perfect Mandarin), I agreed that the Four Seasons had the best ambiance and setup for the size of our event.

Dinner concluded, venue chosen, we finally said our goodbyes in the opulent cream and gold lobby of the Peninsula. I was already counting down the minutes until Ford and I could be alone again.

But of course, Claudia wouldn't stop talking.

She was getting Ford up to speed on all the latest gossip and goings-on of a bunch of their old friends, including a couple of those mean girls who had bullied me back in the day.

"Speaking of which!" she crowed, her big blue eyes lighting up. "Did you know it's Roxana's birthday?"

"Today?" Ford asked. "No way! I haven't seen her since that ski trip we all took a few years back."

"Aspen," Claudia said with a grin. "I know. And yeah, everyone's getting together at the Cubby Bear tonight. We should totally stop by. They'd love to see you."

I looked at my watch pointedly. "I'd actually rather not—"

"I'd love that!" Ford said, drowning me out. "I'll drive. Em?"

Nope. I'd had enough.

"You two go ahead," I said. "I'm sure you'll have a great time."

"Are you sure?" Ford asked, hesitating for the first time all day.

"Honestly—" I started.

"Of course she's sure!" Claudia chirped happily. "She's

an independent woman who can make her own decisions, isn't that right, Emzee?"

Like I could possibly argue with that. "Um, yeah."

Claudia looked triumphant. "See? You have to let her do her own thing, Ford."

Gritting my teeth, I realized I had just given her exactly what she wanted.

"Where did you park?" Claudia was asking, already looping her arm through my husband's and leading him toward the doors.

"Later," I muttered with a half wave.

Slumping into a chair, I watched them walk away. I couldn't believe this was happening. That I was letting Ford go off into the night with my nemesis.

There was only one thing to do now.

I took out my phone and dialed my brother.

"Stefan," I said when he picked up. "Can you send a car for me?"

FORD

CHAPTER 20

Roxana hadn't changed one iota since the last time I'd seen her.

I narrowed my eyes at the birthday girl, who was sitting in the VIP section—or rather, draped across the couch in the VIP section—working on her fifth cocktail of the evening. It was possible she was wearing the same tight-as-hell black bodycon dress I'd last seen her in, and she was definitely getting hammered on the same exact Ciroc & tonics—with the same four lime wedges—she always drank.

As for the rest of the group? Same pretentious jokes about investment banking. Same bragging about their latest luxury vacations abroad. Same rude gossip about the few of our cohort who hadn't been able to come out and celebrate Roxana for one reason or another.

"And that was the last time Ford and I ever set foot in the French Riviera!" Claudia was saying too loudly, squeezing my bicep. "Wasn't it, Ford?"

I hadn't even been paying attention to her story, but everyone else around us was laughing, so all I could do was nod and force a laugh of my own. "That's right."

The whole night I'd felt an overwhelming sense of déjà vu, and not in a good way.

When Claudia had suggested meeting up with the old crew for Roxana's birthday, I'd been thrilled. I'd really thought that getting together with everyone would be a relief. Remind me of simpler times, get my mind off all the bullshit. It had been months since I'd had a proper night out, and I was looking forward to just kicking back with a drink in my hand.

I'd even hoped that a night out apart from Emzee would be a nice break for both of us. A chance to catch our breath. After all, there was a reason for the saying, "absence makes the heart grow fonder," wasn't there? Surely a few hours on our own would be good for both of us.

Hell, maybe my wife would even be jealous enough to make the sex tonight completely over-the-top as compensation. The eye daggers she'd been throwing at Claudia all day hadn't escaped my notice. And I knew the long standing envy that Emzee felt toward my ex hadn't resolved itself much, if at all, since we'd tied the knot.

But instead of giving me an opportunity to relish my temporary freedom or enjoy the company of my old friends, all this evening was doing was making me realize that I wanted something different from my life these days. That now, my idea of a "fun drink" was getting overly tipsy with Emzee on some fancy restaurant's house wine before taking her home to fuck. Not sitting in a loud, overcrowded, "exclusive" club hanging out with a bunch of self-absorbed people who hadn't changed since high school.

That now, my idea of a good conversation involved planning for the future—a future beyond—

"OMG!" Roxana was squealing, reaching across me to take the fresh drink our cocktail waitress had brought over.

"You haven't been to the new resort in Anguilla yet? It's so amazing. You *have* to go! The spa does these gold foil facials..."

"Ahh, incredible. I've been meaning to book it," Claudia said. She kept leaning over me to talk to Roxana, her hand brushing my thigh each time.

I didn't want to be here. I was fucking bored.

Especially with Claudia.

During the tours earlier, I'd had a bit of fun letting her flirt with me. I knew it bugged the shit out of Emzee, but I couldn't resist the ego boost, and watching Claudia fall all over herself for me (after years of unbalanced power dynamics between us and her pulling the stone cold bitch act) was satisfying on some deep level. Plus, I'd figured there was no real harm in it. The flirting wasn't exactly reciprocal on my part, and my marriage was fake, after all.

Now that Emzee was gone, though, I was starting to seriously regret how I'd behaved, because I realized how much her feelings might actually be hurt. And after all my vows to woo her and win her. God, I could be such an ass sometimes.

Not only that, but sitting here surrounded by the old gang, I was also starting to remember exactly how insufferable these social obligations could be—especially with Claudia at my side. My ex had always, always, *always* been more interested in people seeing her as an aspirational figure than in actually being a good person. It was grating on my nerves.

For example, the way she had started off the evening by bragging to the table about how she'd generously donated her time today to help a nonprofit organization that was "simply helpless" at throwing their own fundraiser. It had my stomach turning from the get-go.

And now, she was basically hanging all over me while she gabbed with Roxana, yet she showed absolutely no interest in talking to me, only in being seen with me. I was her accessory for the evening. Or maybe her pet, given the fact that she couldn't stop patting and stroking me like one. Typical Claudia behavior.

It was not cool.

I was so glad to be done with her, done with being treated like a prop. Not that I hadn't done the same to her when we dated. I knew how we'd looked together—we were one of the hot young power couples of Chicago—but like my whole former lifestyle, I was over it. And I was glad I'd only had one drink, hours earlier. Sobriety was really bringing things into sharp focus.

"Claudia," I said, peeling her hand off my arm to get her attention.

She was giggling away with Roxana, who looked like she was about one Ciroc and tonic away from sliding onto the floor and passing out.

"*Claudia*," I said again, firmly enough that she leaned back with an annoyed look.

"What?"

"I need to talk to you. Privately," I told her.

"Perfect!" she said, brightening. "Let's take a picture together. We'd get so many likes."

Just another reminder that the rest of the world was nothing more than a backdrop for her social media accounts. She probably only wanted to post a photo so Emzee would see it.

There was no way I could stand another five minutes with Claudia, let alone the countless minutes it would take her to get a good enough photo. That's how we'd spent all of our trips. Capturing the best-looking moments for Claudia to flaunt later. They were never planned around what we wanted to see, but where she wanted to *be* seen.

"I'm not taking a picture with you," I told her flatly, steering her into a semi-quiet corner near the club's restrooms.

She pouted. She was still beautiful when she pouted (I had always theorized that it was something she'd perfected by practicing in the mirror), but I was immune to that now.

"Oh, come on," she said. "Emzee's not here. You don't have to pretend with me."

"Pretend what?"

"That you don't like this." She leaned in, her lips brushing my ear as her hand slid up over my chest.

"Claudia, you have to stop flirting with me," I said, gently pushing her away.

She laughed. "Why? You love it when I'm all over you," she said. "Especially in public, so everyone can see how good we look together."

Once upon a time, she would have been correct. This was exactly how we used to act when we were out in public together. I'd liked people knowing that I was fucking someone as beautiful and well regarded as Claudia, and she liked people knowing that she was dating someone as wealthy and well-connected as me. It had been a mutually beneficial arrangement.

Until it wasn't anymore.

"You and I aren't together anymore, Claudia," I chastised her. "I'm a married man. You need to respect that."

Instead of taking me seriously, she put her hand back on my chest and let out a fake-sounding laugh, waving at Roxana across the club as if the two of us were having some great conversation, not an awkward argument. Typical Claudia. Again.

I pried her hand off me, huffing a sigh of annoyance. "I'm with my *wife* now. Okay?"

"Are you, really?" She leaned back and narrowed her eyes at me, making true eye contact for the first time since we'd walked through the door of the club. "Because...you aren't with your wife now. You're with *me*."

And for the first time, I saw exactly what Claudia was seeing.

She was right.

I'd fucked up.

I stood there, surrounded by loud music and overpriced cocktails and people I barely knew anymore—people I didn't really like, if I was honest—and let the realization sink in.

Claudia had played me.

Or rather, I'd fucking played myself.

Yeah, I had hoped to make Emzee jealous, but maybe I had gone too far. In fact, now that I really thought about it, the look on her face in the lobby of the Peninsula had been a little too cheery to be real. And yeah, I'd better go home and fix this. Stat.

I looked at Claudia, took in the smug, self-satisfied smirk, the raised brow.

"You're right," I told her. "I should be with my wife. I'm leaving."

"*What?*" My words were clearly not what she'd been expecting.

"See you around," I said.

I strode out of the club, not even stopping by the table to say goodbye to anyone else.

Once the valet brought my car around, I took off, tires screeching. The entire drive home, I racked my brain for ways I could make this up to Emzee, for all the ways I could apologize. Flowers, maybe, definitely a nice dinner out. Maybe take Munchkin for a doggie spa day.

When I got back to the apartment, I took a deep breath, unlocked the front door, and...found the place dark and quiet.

I figured Emzee had just gone to bed, but I didn't hear Munchkin either. Usually he would come out to greet me, tail wagging, no matter how late it was.

Nothing.

"Em? Emzee?" I called out.

I went into the bedroom and found the bed still made from earlier this morning. Then I checked the guest room. Empty. The office. Empty. The whole apartment was empty.

All that remained was a note that I finally found stuck to the fridge with a magnet.

Going to a business convention in NY with my brothers, it said. *Munchkin staying with Brooklyn for the weekend. Back on Monday. –MZ*

My wife was gone, and she'd taken the dog with her.

EMZEE

CHAPTER 21

Since Ford had no problem ditching me to go party it up with Claudia and the mean girls, I figured I might as well do my own thing too and be with the people I loved most—my family.

But it just so happened that my brothers were spending the weekend at the Borderless Business Convention in New York. So that was where I had ended up.

After Ford had taken Claudia's arm and left me in the lobby of the Peninsula Hotel, I'd called Stefan and jumped into action. By the time I'd packed myself a bag and gathered up Munchkin to drop off with Brooklyn, Stefan's assistant had already booked me a late flight into JFK and a hotel room at the convention center.

I arrived at the hotel with just enough time to shower and roll into bed, completely exhausted. The next morning I took advantage of a quick room service breakfast and then headed down to the convention floor to meet my brothers.

"Glad you could make it," Stefan said, giving me a quick squeeze before handing me my nametag lanyard. "Nice suit by the way."

"Thanks. It's Alexander McQueen." This was my first big business convention, and I was relieved the dark plaid met with his approval.

"Rock'n'roll aesthetic on point as usual," Luka said as we strolled past the booths. "What made you change your mind about the convention?"

Shrugging, I fibbed, "Just thought it would be good to do a little networking outside of the greater Chicago area. Plus, it's New York. You know I'm mostly here for the pizza."

They laughed, and we got into a brief but heated debate over the merits of Chicago deep dish vs. New York style pies. It was great seeing them, even though I knew I'd probably be on my own for most of the day.

After making loose dinner plans, we split up. Just as I'd suspected, they both had lots of meetings and seminars on their schedules and all the usual industry people to visit with. Meanwhile, I was tasked with exploring the convention floor to suss out if there were any new connections to be made—particularly outside of the agenting world, since Danica Rose already had those networks covered.

At first, I felt pretty useless.

By 9 a.m., the convention center was packed. I was doing everything I could to fend off my anxiety as I wove my way down rows of buzzing booths, reminding myself to smile at every passing stranger. Large, noisy crowds always made me feel small. Like I was an awkward teenager in school again, wondering if every aside or giggle was about me.

What made it even harder to concentrate on my deep breathing (and generally acting professional) was that all I could think about was Ford. How his night out with Claudia had gone, and whether he'd even made it home afterward. Maybe they hadn't even made it to the bar for

Roxana's birthday. Maybe the "birthday" was just an excuse for them to run off together.

Trying to shake off my worries, I dragged myself to the keynote address. Then I went to a panel on search engine optimization, after which I wolfed down a bagel in the food court while checking my phone for the umpteenth time, but of course there was still nothing from Ford.

Why hadn't he called or texted me by now, even just to say he'd gotten my note? What was he doing? I was sick at the possibility that he'd slept with Claudia—and that I was at least partly to blame.

Had I done the wrong thing by leaving town? Had I pushed my husband and his ex back together by refusing to be a part of Ford's lifestyle? I still couldn't believe how brazen Claudia had been in her flirting—but the thing that really hurt was how Ford hadn't seemed to mind at all. And how, ultimately, it didn't matter how flirty they'd gotten or how inappropriate their behavior was. Because Ford wasn't really mine.

I needed to get that through my head once and for all.

Okay. Chin up. Time to focus on the task at hand: promoting Danica Rose. Not zoning out during every seminar I could duck into and mooning over my fake husband.

Or maybe I should just track down my brothers and see about tagging along with them. That would keep me on my toes. I'd just step out to the lobby and give Stefan a call.

Whipping around abruptly, I walked right into someone, bouncing off a hard male chest.

"Well, if it isn't the last person I expected to bump into here," an amused voice said. "You okay?"

I looked up—right into the deep blue eyes of Andrew

Apellido, of *lookingglass* magazine. "Andrew!" I exclaimed, immediately comforted by his familiar face. "How are you?"

"Even better than I was five seconds ago," he said. "Delighted to see you, Emzee."

He gave me a hug and I returned it, though I wondered if his excitement in seeing me wasn't solely because he was interested in talking business.

"You should have told me you were in New York," he said. "There's nothing I love more than showing off my city to people from out of town."

"It was a last-minute decision," I said. "I didn't know I was coming until last night."

"A great decision, in my opinion," he said. "These conferences are always hit or miss, but when you have the right person to explore them with, they can be a whole lot of fun."

"Oh yeah?" I said. "Prove it. I'm totally overwhelmed."

Andrew grinned. "See now, we can easily fix that. Drink? The lobby bar is great."

If I couldn't save my marriage or even my relationship with Ford, I was at least going to do what I could to keep my professional career afloat. Plus, I liked the guy.

"I'm in," I said.

I was grateful to get out of the crowd and retreat to the bar, which was much quieter and calmer than I'd expected.

"My brothers love your magazine," I told Andrew once we'd gotten our drinks.

"I appreciate it," he said. "But I'm much more interested in hearing what *you* think about my magazine."

He was clearly flirting, but he also seemed genuinely interested.

"I'm a fan," I said. "From what I've seen, I think it has a lot of potential. Beyond just the images, the articles are thought provoking, almost like what *Playboy* used to publish. It could really make some waves, depending on what direction you take it in."

"That's the million-dollar question, isn't it?" He took a sip of his drink, a simple tequila on the rocks. "My goal is to create the kind of magazine that everyone talks about. Publish work that's risky—to shock and inspire our readers, make sure we're a magazine everyone knows."

"I'm into that," I said. It aligned exactly with the vision I had for my own work. I craved the freedom to push boundaries, to try new things without fearing rejection from the mainstream.

"I want us to tackle the tough issues!" Andrew went on. "Not shy away from discussing what's controversial or intense. I want to be controversial. How would you like to spend thirty days documenting the effects of climate change right here in America's backyards, for instance?"

Nodding, I said, "Love to. It's too easy for people to ignore photos of melting icebergs."

"Exactly! You have to be more immediate. Get in people's faces a little bit, or a lot."

I was so inspired by his words, my mind had already begun churning with all the ways I could contribute.

"My brother was floored by the piece about European influence here in the States," I said. "Photo essays have the potential for *incredible* impact. Have you thought about pairing writers and photographers together during development? To make the projects more cohesive."

Andrew looked at me intently. "You know, what I really need is a photography editor-in-chief of sorts, someone who understands the role of images in storytelling. Who can work closely with me to make sure the visual needs of our stories are met."

My stomach was doing little somersaults. It was as if Andrew had just created my dream job out of nowhere. The thought of working with writers and photographers to craft narratives was exactly the kind of thing I was passionate about.

"What else are you thinking?" he asked before ordering us another round of drinks.

I pulled out my phone. I didn't want to obsess, but I couldn't stop myself—nothing from Ford. I tried to ignore my disappointment as I pulled up the magazine's Instagram feed.

"You could be doing so much more with your social media presence," I told him.

"Sure, of course." He leaned forward to look at my screen. "Like what?"

"For one," I said, "you should divide your Instagram feed. One can be devoted to promoting the articles, as it is now. But then another should be purely photo. Eye candy."

I almost volunteered to manage it, but caught myself before I could offer. No matter what was happening with me and Ford, I'd agreed to stay married to him for at least a year and I was going to stick to that promise. No relocating to New York just yet.

But that didn't mean I couldn't start planting the seeds for the future.

"Brilliant," Andrew said. "You really know your stuff."

"I just love photography," I said.

I reached to take my phone back, but he was looking at my own IG account now. It was mostly travel photos, beautiful plates of food, and Munchkin.

"Ever thought about taking your own advice?" Andrew said with a smile. "Don't get me wrong, these are great—but you could be showing off your real work on your page. Go public."

He was right. I *should* post more of my professional work on social media, for the whole world to see. But I always hesitated. I worried my life would start revolving around the number of likes and comments I managed to get, and the possibility of getting trolled or harassed.

"I'll think about it," I said, trying to deflect.

"Seriously," he said, his voice going softer. "What kind of photos would you want to fill your account with? If you knew nobody would judge you?"

"Hmm," I said, sipping my drink while I mulled it over. "I think I'd put up photos I've done during my off hours. I work with a lot of beautiful models, but I like showing them in a different light. Not just shooting them for the sake of a pretty picture. Some of them have the most incredible bone structure. I like exploring different kinds of beauty, I guess."

"I love that," Andrew said, completely rapt.

I knew I might be crossing a line, continuing to engage with him—especially since our conversation was moving away from the magazine and work—but I needed the distraction. Andrew wasn't taking my mind off of Ford entirely, but at least I had something to do.

After all, my brothers were still busy schmoozing and making contacts with people who might be able to help Danica Rose, leaving me to fend for myself. Or maybe this conversation with Andrew was exactly the kind of networking that Stefan and Luka wanted me to be doing.

Andrew looked at his watch. We'd been at the bar for a few hours already, talking and nursing our drinks.

"Gosh, I'm sorry," I said. "I didn't realize how late it was getting. I'm totally monopolizing you."

"Not at all. Would you like to continue this conversation over dinner? My treat."

"I'd love to," I said, telling myself it was still all about business—because it was, right?

And even if it wasn't, it didn't matter what Andrew wanted out of it. I was going in a purely professional capacity. I shouldn't have to feel guilty. Ford going out with Claudia sure as hell hadn't been business.

First, though, I needed to get ready and text my brothers to let them know I wouldn't be meeting back up with them.

"I should change," I said. "I've been sweating in this wool suit all day."

"Good idea," he said as we paid our tabs. "Let me walk you to your room and I can pick you back up in an hour or so."

As we rode up to my floor in the elevator, we talked more about the power of Instagram.

"People scroll through their feeds so mindlessly now, you have to grab them as quickly as possible," I said. "Every image has to be its own story."

Andrew nodded and I could tell he was listening, but I also knew that he was focused on what would happen at my hotel room door. If I asked him to, he'd probably come right on in. All I had to do was give him a sign that I was interested.

The elevator dinged and the doors slid open. I hesitated.

"Shall we?" he said.

"Right. I'm just at the end of the hall," I said.

We headed toward my door, and I could feel a subtle tension building between us. I couldn't help fantasizing about how different it would be to kiss a man who was actually interested in me. Who wasn't doing it because of some stupid hoax. Who wanted to kiss me because I was me. Not because I was the solution to some problem he had.

But even in my fantasy, and even with Andrew right in front of me, when I imagined kissing him, he ended up looking like Ford.

We reached my room. I slid my keycard into the reader, and the green light blinked. Andrew was lingering just a little too close.

"I'll, umm, see you soon?" I said, looking up.

And that was when he made his move.

Leaning in, it was obvious he meant to kiss me. Without even asking. Startled, I put my hand on his chest to push him away.

It was at that exact moment that the door—*my* hotel room door—opened.

"What the fuck is going on here?"

I turned and found Ford standing in the threshold of my room.

Had he seriously flown to New York to surprise me?

Well, I was definitely surprised.

And I wasn't the only one.

FORD

CHAPTER 22

There wasn't enough time to savor the "I told you so" moment in my head before I realized it was Andrew Homewrecker Apellido who was moving in on my wife.

Nor was there enough time to fully enjoy the look of total shock and awe on that slimy asshole's face when he realized what was happening.

As he stood there in the hallway gawping at me, my fist went flying. Straight for Andrew's face, and practically of its own accord. It wasn't even planned. I punched the guy purely on instinct, and damn did it feel good.

"Ford!" Emzee cried out.

Andrew staggered back, stunned. "You son of a—"

He lunged forward to throw his own punch. It hit me square in the jaw.

Which was unexpected, truth be told. But fun. Because a good fight was exactly what I needed right now.

"Andrew!" Emzee scolded. "Both of you, stop!"

Our blood was up, adrenaline pumping. Neither of us paid her any mind.

Andrew swung again but I twisted out of the way just in time, then delivered my own shot to the gut, which had him gasping. When he threw an elbow, it knocked me backward into the hotel room. He charged in after me like a raging bull, wrapping his arms around my waist and trying to knock me down.

Instead, I used his momentum to shove him into the desk—a desk I'd spent the last few hours fantasizing about fucking my wife on top of—and then leaned over him to see if he was still conscious. That was when his fist came up and connected with my brow bone.

I barely registered what was happening. Everything was a blur of pain and triumph as we rolled around on the floor trading blows.

My frustration and rage, my disappointment, the pressure to succeed and the ever-looming fear of failing—my marriage, my job, my parents, my ex-girlfriend—all my warring emotions and the things in my life that I couldn't control were boiling over inside me. Fueling me. It didn't matter that Andrew Apellido himself had little to do with my problems.

In the background, I could still faintly hear Emzee yelling at us to stop, and I wasn't entirely sure whose blood was on my shirt, but it wasn't until Andrew held his hands up and stopped fighting that I finally stopped, too.

Both of us were panting and disheveled, furniture was upturned, a smear of blood marred the cream and gold pattern of the carpet. My anger was fading, but Andrew had gotten some pretty good shots in. My face throbbed, and every muscle in my body ached.

"*Gentlemen,*" a sharp female voice said.

Our heads swiveled toward the doorway, where the

very unamused hotel manager and a few burly security guards were looming.

"I've come to escort you out of my hotel," she said, sounding for all the world like a harried elementary school principal. "Your transportation to Urgent Care awaits."

Andrew held up a hand. "Ma'am, I really don't think it's necessary—"

"Unless you'd prefer I have the *police* take you there," the manager finished.

That was when I started to come back to my senses.

Behind the manager, I could see into the hallway, where Emzee stood glaring down at me with her arms folded over her chest. Even angry as hell, my wife was beautiful. And even knowing I was in deep shit with her, I couldn't help smiling a little.

"To tell you the truth, jail time might be preferable to whatever my wife has in store for me," I joked as I dragged myself up off the carpet.

Nobody laughed, and all I saw was a scowl on Emzee's face as she stepped aside to make way for me and Andrew and the phalanx of guards separating us.

It wasn't until all three of us were loaded into the van headed for the Urgent Care—Andrew in the passenger seat, Emzee in the second row, and me in the far back—that I fully realized exactly what I'd done.

Beyond the physical fight and all the pain that came with it, I felt a mixture of shame for losing control and regret for upsetting Emzee, who so far had refused to look at me or even acknowledge my presence during the ride.

Up in the passenger seat, I could make out Andrew holding his wadded-up necktie to his bleeding lip. Looking at him made me realize that I was still angry, too. How dare that douchebag attempt to move in on my girl. I curled my hands into fists and winced as I grasped the fact that I'd fucked up royally as well.

In fact, the more I examined it, the more obvious it became that I was mostly angry at myself. At the fact that my brilliant plan to win Emzee hadn't been convincing enough for the rest of the world to see it. I'd told myself that I was going to do whatever it took to make her mine, and this was what had happened. Obviously, my ploy had been fucking useless if someone like Andrew had felt like he could make a move.

Because he never would have tried to shoot his shot if he didn't think the basket was open.

And if I had thought Emzee was mad at me before over the whole Claudia thing, well, that was absolutely nothing compared to how furious she was right now.

We arrived at Urgent Care and she didn't even spare me a backward glance before helping Andrew out of the van and walking him inside. When I followed, she spoke to the nurse on call, making sure he knew that both of us needed medical attention, but she avoided my gaze the entire time. Once we were both checked in, she went with Andrew to his exam room and left me to wait for the doctor by myself.

I couldn't help wondering if I had really, truly fucked this up for good.

I'd seen the way she had been caring for Andrew. Maybe this guy *was* the one she really wanted. Maybe if I hadn't convinced her to get involved in this whole fake marriage scheme, she would actually be out dating and meeting someone like Andrew.

After all, what had *I* done for Emzee?

All I'd done was lead her further and further along a path she asked not to be on in the first place. Meanwhile,

Andrew had already expressed interest in her work and career, offering her a job in a field that she loved. He'd been there for her when she needed to leave Chicago, and he'd even walked her up to her hotel room. That was something I wasn't always allowed to do.

The doctor came in, clearing her throat as she flipped through my intake forms.

"Got into a bit of an altercation, did we?" she said.

"You should see the other guy," I joked weakly.

"Oh, I did," she said, chuckling as she clicked a small flashlight. "Can you look toward the light, please? Just want to be sure you're not concussed."

After a brief exam, a nurse came in to administer a round of stinging antiseptic and gauze. I was also told that I'd need to get a few stitches above my eye.

As the doctor began to stitch me up, I realized that I had been a giant, unfair shit when it came to Emzee.

Our fake marriage had always had an expiration date attached to it. That was the deal. But I hadn't thought much about what would happen to Emzee after it was all over. I had safety nets and fallback plans. I even had a fucking fall-back wife—Claudia—if I wanted one.

What did Emzee have?

She'd accused me before of cockblocking her future, which I hadn't agreed with at the time. Now I could see that in a way, she was right. Despite the fact that things had shifted over the course of our relationship (fake or not), that both of us had changed, I was still acting like it was a given that Emzee saw me as her superior. Her hero. That whatever I needed, whatever I wanted, I could get from her with minimal effort on my part.

I expected her to be happy just to get crumbs of my attention and affection, the way she had been in high school. I'd even spent half a day flirting with Claudia right in front of her, like a total jackass, not realizing until later what it must have felt like for Emzee to have to see me and my ex together. I'd been so focused on my own shit that I hadn't stopped to consider the consequences of what I was doing to Emzee and how it was going to affect her—not just now, but even after our marriage was over.

During the last seven years, I couldn't remember a time where I hadn't somehow held her back. Over and over I had proven that I wasn't listening, that I was only focused on myself and my needs.

Well. I was done with all of that now.

It was time to stop standing in her way.

EMZEE

CHAPTER 23

Back in the hotel room, I was so angry I could barely see straight.

Thanks to Ford, we'd been officially kicked out by the manager, so now we were packing up. I had no idea if Ford was flying back to Chicago right away or not, but my plan was to head to the hotel across the street, where my brother had luckily secured me a last-minute reservation. I'd texted with him and Luka earlier, giving them the least embarrassing version of the "my jealous husband got in a fistfight with Andrew Apellido" story I could manage. They'd been pretty understanding, but I was still humiliated.

As I stormed out of the bathroom with my toiletry case, I shot Ford a glare. He was brooding, barely speaking or even looking in my direction as he zipped up his laptop bag and set it on his suitcase. He'd been that way since we got back from Urgent Care.

I was sick and tired of it.

It was bad enough that I felt guilty for spending the day with Andrew, even though we'd done nothing wrong.

Having Ford sulk around like he thought I owed him an apology was just icing on the cake. I wasn't the one responsible for our current plight.

We'd just spent several long hours at a walk-in clinic, where poor Andrew got stitches in his lip, a splint for a broken finger, and was checked for a concussion. The whole time I'd been sitting with him, I couldn't stop apologizing for what had happened. Ford had really gone off the deep end—he should be grateful Andrew wasn't pressing charges.

Part of me couldn't deny that there was something hot (in a primal, caveman-like way) about Ford trying to defend my honor...but that didn't change the fact that the violence had been completely unnecessary. And stupidly bloody. I had already rejected Andrew's kiss, which my husband would have known if he hadn't just flung open the door, jumped to conclusions, and sucker punched the guy in the face. If he had stopped for one moment and given me a chance to explain, we could have avoided the whole thing.

So yeah. Ford was the one at fault. I didn't need him acting like I was the guilty party.

What the hell was he even doing in New York to begin with? Did he really not trust me at a business conference with my brothers? The irony was, I never would have left Chicago, wouldn't have even come to this convention, wouldn't have run into Andrew *at all*, if Ford hadn't ditched me to go out with Claudia and their old crew.

Sinking onto the bed, I looked at my husband. "I'm going to the hotel across the street. Stefan got me a room there. Are you coming?"

Wordlessly, he nodded. We made the trek in silence.

By the time I had checked in and we had taken the elevator up and dropped our bags down in the new room, I couldn't take the tension between us any longer. As he started unpacking his work bag on the desk, I waited for him to say something. Anything. To apologize, or at least explain himself. But no.

When he was done, he sat down in the desk chair and rotated to face me. Still saying nothing. Like he expected *me* to apologize.

Filled with resentment, I exploded.

"Okay, what is your problem? Is this about our marriage? Is it because I was on my way to a business dinner with Andrew? How is any of this fair? *You're* the one who roped me into this whole charade to begin with. First it was fake dating, then it was a fake engagement, and now it's a fake marriage. Except, surprise! We're really married now. And all because you didn't want to deal with your parents pushing you to marry Claudia—"

"Emzee—" he interrupted, slumped in the desk chair.

"No! *I'm* speaking!" I interrupted right back. "You acted like it was do or die trying to get away from your ex, but then you let her flirt with you in front of me for an entire day—which you knew I didn't like but which you were clearly enjoying—and then you left me and went out with her.

"So yes, I came here to this convention. To remind myself that I'm my own person, and to maybe try to figure out what I'm going to do with my life after our divorce. But then you just pop up out of nowhere to sabotage me and punch my potential future employer in the face! And now *you're* the broody one? Really? Ha!

"*I* should be the one pouting and slamming closet doors and refusing to look you in the eye, not the other way around."

Losing steam, I finally stopped yelling and stalked over

to the window. The lights of New York did nothing to calm me.

"You have every right to be upset," Ford said quietly, having the nerve to sound remorseful. Or maybe it was a ploy for sympathy. "I just want—"

I was furious all over again, and nowhere near ready to hear his side.

"No, Ford," I said, whirling around to face him. "You know what your problem is? It's that you have *no idea* what you want. You're trying to keep all of your own options open, while ensuring that no one else has any other option but you. I can see right through you."

Stopping to catch my breath, I pushed away the feelings of tenderness I felt when I looked at my husband's stitched-up eyebrow and gauze-wrapped knuckles. I knew he'd be hurting tomorrow, but I told myself he had more than earned his bruises. Ford's injuries were Ford's fault. He had left Andrew far worse, and deserved whatever pain he got.

"I know what I want," he muttered.

"Oh really," I scoffed, still burning up. "Tell me something, Ford. Why did you even come here?"

Despite my confrontational tone, my bravado, my anger, all of it—I was scared to hear his reply. I wanted to know the answer, yes, but I was also afraid that I already knew what it was.

That he'd flown to New York to tell me he wanted a divorce, sooner than the year we'd agreed upon. So that he could marry Claudia, or at least be free to sleep with whomever he wanted. It was the only answer that made sense, and I could feel my heart pounding in my chest as I waited for him to confirm what I already knew.

He didn't say anything for a while, looking down at the carpet and shaking his head.

I've heard that your life flashes before your eyes at the instant of your death, and I was definitely experiencing some of that now. Not my whole life, just my life with Ford. Probably because this was the instant of our relationship's death.

I recalled in vivid detail the first time he'd come to my rescue, during sophomore year at Wayland-Blaine. It was in study hall, this jackass named Blake calling me a whore. Ford had swooped in and I'd felt so relieved, so protected.

Or the time he'd brought me to some jock's pool party when we were juniors, and how during spin the bottle, I'd run from the room when the bottle I had spun landed on Ford and I was too overwhelmed to go through with the kiss in front of everyone. I'd cried myself to sleep that night, regretting my cowardice. Convinced it was the only chance I would ever get to kiss Ford Malone. And that I'd totally blown it.

The care packages I'd sent to him every month while we were away at college across the country from each other— me in art school and him studying business. I'd pack those boxes with junk food, homemade cookies, Christmas decorations, coloring books, party favors, puzzles, the cheesy paperback detective novels that he loved. Anything to perk him up and give him a break from all the studying and the very un-fun classes I knew he was hating, which he'd complain about during our hours-long phone calls.

The sex we'd had on our honeymoon, or at the beach on Martha's Vineyard. The night I'd given my virginity to him.

The times I'd caught him napping on the couch with Munchkin tucked against him, both of them snoring away. Melting my heart like butter on a griddle.

Our breakfasts together. Our lazy Sundays.

And his beautiful proposal in the botanic gardens—the

one that turned out to be an ambush, all for show...yet that had seemed so sincere in the moments before all our friends and family jumped out of the bushes yelling, "Surprise!"

All of it—our past, our present, our future—meant nothing now.

Ford stood up, walking closer to me. I looked him in the eye, mouth in a firm line, steeling myself for the worst.

"I came here because...because it's you," he said.

"What?" I sputtered, completely lost.

Ford sighed. "It's you, Em. *You're* what I want. You're why I came."

EMZEE

CHAPTER 24

"I—I don't understand," I said. It was the only thing I could think to say.

Because yes, I'd always longed to hear him say those words—but why now? What did he really want? What did he really mean?

"I think you do," Ford said.

"Say it again," I whispered.

He moved closer, locking eyes with me. "I want *you*. No one else."

Okay, but...what exactly did he want me *for*? To recommit to the ruse, renegotiate the terms of our contract? Maybe he wanted more PDA, more publicity—to grant media interviews like Luka and Stefan had with their wives. Pose for pictures with Munchkin, give Ford a chance to up his PR status to boost Malone Real Estate Holdings in the public eye.

Shaking my head, I said, "No more games. Whatever else you're trying to get out of me, out of this agreement, just say it."

"Em." Ford stepped in front of me, so close I could feel

the heat from his body. Feel myself responding to his near-ness, the way I always had. My heart pounding, my knees gone weak, my cheeks flushing with warmth. "I want to be with you. That's all."

"You...want to be with me..." I murmured, trying to comprehend.

He grinned. "And now who's the one who wants to keep their options open? But we've got time. Kiss me better, now."

Wait. *What?* My brow furrowed. Was Ford implying... that he was recommitting to *us*? As a real couple? Did he seriously mean it? God, I hoped so.

"Where does it hurt?" I asked, eyeing the stitches over his eyebrow. I gently took his head in my hands and tilted his face down to kiss his cheekbone, his temple, his forehead above the wound.

"Much further south, I think," he said, attempting a wink and then wincing at the effort.

I couldn't help laughing at him, and he chuckled along with me.

"You are an idiot," I said affectionately.

"I'm your idiot," he said with a shrug.

The tension and frustration and heaviness between us seemed to lift, and we both relaxed a little. Maybe this was exactly the kind of turning-point conflict we had needed. Something to test our bond, our partnership. If so, maybe all the bullshit had been worth it.

"Much further south, huh?" I asked, glancing down. "I think I can help." I gave him a sultry look before sinking down onto my knees.

"Emzee," he groaned.

I unbuttoned his pants, feeling the press of his cock against my fingers as I lowered the zipper. Tugging his briefs down, I released him. As I'd suspected, he was already fully hard. With a smirk, I grazed the tip with my tongue.

"Fuck yes," Ford murmured, digging his hands into my hair to cup the back of my head.

Pulling back, I stroked him, my fist tight around his hard cock.

There was a drop of precum at the head, and I leaned forward to lick it clean. Ford's fingers tightened and he let out a groan.

"Fuck me," he sighed. "Fuck me with your mouth."

I wanted to, but I also didn't want to rush. I took it slow, dragging my tongue over the head of his cock with long, slow licks. I wet my hand, dragging it over the ridges of his shaft, my spit creating a lubricant that made the slide of my palm easier. Smoother. As I pumped the base of his cock with my hand, I opened my mouth wide and took him deep into my mouth.

"Fuck," he gasped. "Just like that. That's what I want."

I took him even deeper, relaxing my throat as much as possible, my mouth and hand working in tandem as I sucked him off with everything I could muster. Soon, Ford's hips began to thrust and I braced myself, my knees on the floor, my hands on his hips as he began to fuck my mouth, gripping the back of my head to steady himself.

He was groaning above me, mouth open, eyes closed. "Your mouth feels so good. Your hot, wet mouth. I love fucking it, just like I love fucking your hot, wet pussy."

I was aching at his words, getting wetter and hotter by the second. I loved the feel of him fucking my mouth, the power I felt, but I wanted more of him.

Without warning, he pulled me to my feet, his tongue in my mouth. He grunted at first contact—the cut on his lip had to be painful still—but it didn't seem to deter him in the slightest.

His hands were everywhere. In my hair, up my shirt, down my pants. And then he was walking me backward to the bed, guiding me until I felt the mattress hit the back of my legs. With a push, Ford tossed me down. As I gazed hungrily up at him, he narrowed his eyes at me, his cock, still wet from my mouth, standing at attention.

"You're looking very overdressed, Mrs. Malone."

Smirking, I said, "Am I?"

"Take off your clothes," he ordered. "All of them. Slowly."

I sat up and obeyed, watching him strip down almost as slowly as I was.

When I was down to nothing but my black thong, he shook his head.

"I changed my mind," he said.

Placing his knee on the bed, he leaned over and ran his hand up the outside of my leg, his fingers coming to rest on the waistband on my thong. Then he looped his thumb into it and gave it a rough tug. I heard a rip and the whole thing came apart in his hand.

I smiled as he tossed the ruined lace thong away. "You're a brute," I teased.

"Spread your legs," he said. "I'm going to make you come so hard, you'll forget every other man on earth."

My pulse doubled. "I don't doubt that."

Ford put his hands on my knees and spread my legs even wider before settling between them. "That's a pretty pussy," he groaned, his fingers tracing the wetness there.

I closed my eyes as he teased me, his touch soft and gentle, making me pant.

"Ford, please," I begged. "You're torturing me."

"You want me to fuck you?"

"Yes. Please."

"I need to taste you first," he said, lowering his head.

His tongue traced the length of my slit, slow and deep, circled my clit, and then dipped back down and then up again. It was almost enough to make me come already. I gripped the back of his head, fingers tight in his hair as his tongue pushed deeper inside me. I moaned louder.

"Mmm," he groaned, the vibrations pushing me even closer to the edge.

He began tongue-fucking me, spearing me with heat and wetness, teasing my clit with his thumb. The sensations were almost too much to handle.

Suddenly he switched it up, his tongue moving to play with my clit as his fingers took over stroking inside me, stretching me wider as I lifted my hips to meet each thrust.

"Ford," I panted. "I'm going to come."

"Mm-hmm," Ford hummed again, and the vibrations made my toes curl.

Without warning, my orgasm crashed into me. My entire body shuddered, my pussy clenching around Ford's fingers, the pleasure washing over me in hot waves.

I was still moaning as Ford rose up on his knees, spreading my legs even wider as he pressed his cock against my slick opening. He moved more stiffly than usual, and I could see a dark bruise along his ribcage, but he clearly wasn't going to let his injuries keep him from doing exactly what he wanted. Me.

"You want this cock?" he demanded.

He slipped the head of his cock inside me, but didn't go any further. Then he was moving just a little, teasing me with it, making me cry out.

"More," I pled.

I expected him to give me what I wanted, but instead he leaned over me, still barely inside me, and laced our fingers together. His eyes were on mine, his gaze unwavering.

"I want you, Em," he said. "All of you."

Then, without looking away, he pushed slowly into me, hard and deep, deeper than he'd ever gone before. With a gasp I squeezed his hands tighter, searching his eyes, feeling more bonded to him than I ever had before. Our bodies fit together perfectly, a key in a lock. Our connection felt so intense and so intimate that I was blinking back tears.

"Em," Ford moaned, starting to thrust faster, and I could see that he was equally overwhelmed by what was happening.

His mouth dropped onto mine, his kiss searing, searching, and I closed my eyes at the pleasure of it all, my head going back. I savored the feel of his cock, the slide of our tongues, the warmth of his skin against mine.

"Fuck," he groaned, and I opened my eyes again.

He was watching my face, our hands still linked. Then he pulled out slowly, withdrawing almost completely before pumping back into me, so deep it sent a shock of pleasure through me that had both of us crying out.

"You like that?" he asked.

I nodded, and he kept on fucking me like that—slowly, sensually—our fingers laced together, our eyes never leaving each other. The rest of the world slipped away. Everything was Ford. I didn't think about the deal we'd made, the lies we'd told. I didn't think about Claudia or Andrew or the Malones or my brothers. I didn't think about DRM or the Bratva.

I didn't think about everything we still had to overcome.

Because in this moment, what we had...it felt real.

Pleasure built inside me with each of Ford's thrusts. My

legs were spread wide, my body open completely to him as the sounds of our moans echoed in the room. With one hand still linked in mine, Ford slid his other palm under my ass, lifting me up, tilting my hips so he could go even deeper. It was as if he was touching my heart with his body.

I wanted to do the same, and I squeezed my pussy around his thick cock, wanting to be closer to him, wanting us to come together. I was close, and I could tell he was too.

Ford let out a gasp as I squeezed him, my body meeting each of his thrusts with a tight vise. He started fucking me faster and faster, his eyes never leaving mine as his movements became wild, his grunts louder, clutching my hand even tighter as he pushed us toward the edge.

As I started to come, I pulled his body down onto me, clinging to his broad shoulders as the pleasure radiated from my core, my pussy contracting around his cock.

"Come with me," I begged. He nodded.

Ford's eyes stayed on mine as he reached his climax, cursing under his breath as he spilled his hot seed inside me, shuddering as he filled me up. And then we were kissing again, our bodies tangling as we held each other tight, our hands still linked.

EMZEE

CHAPTER 25

I'd set my alarm early so I'd have enough time to shower and pack and join my brothers on their chartered flight back home to Chicago. But when it went off, and it was still dark out, I couldn't make myself get up. Especially with Ford curled up in bed beside me.

Luckily, I didn't have much time to consider my options. Ford had already reached over and turned off the alarm, pulling me into his arms.

Well.

With that decision made, I snuggled into his embrace and fell back asleep.

Hours later, I woke up again—this time with Ford's head between my thighs, his thumb pressed against my clit, his tongue lapping me up.

"Mmm," I murmured, spreading my legs wider. "Good morning."

I fisted the sheets as his mouth worked me hard, trying to relax as the pleasure coursed through me. There were plenty of worse ways to be woken up.

Soon enough, he was fucking me with his fingers,

sucking my clit as his hand stretched my already sore body. After the workout he gave me last night, it should have felt like too much, but it didn't. I came faster than I would have liked but not too hard, moaning dreamily.

It was the best kind of morning.

Or was it afternoon already? Once I recovered from my unexpected wake-up orgasm, I rolled over and turned my phone back on, finding a few texts from my brothers waiting for me.

Assuming you're catching a flight back with Mr. Jealous, Luka had texted. *But lmk if you get stuck and we'll book something for you asap. This is a judgment-free zone.*

And from Stefan: *Talk soon and good luck with Ford. Call if you need anything.*

I sent a group text so my brothers would know I was safe with Ford and apologized for missing the flight, letting them know I had simply slept in. I reassured them I'd be home soon and then sat up on the edge of the bed, stretching luxuriously.

The bedside clock said it was just past 10:30, which was a hell of a lot later than I usually got up but technically still counted as "morning"—which was good enough for me. Plus, it felt nice to sleep in. I couldn't even be mad that Ford had shut off my phone to let me rest.

"I know you were planning to go back to Chicago with your brothers today," Ford said, not looking even a little guilty about changing my plans by shutting my alarm off. "But I have another plan."

I raised my eyebrow. I tried to be annoyed that he had made plans without consulting me, but it was nearly impossible to mad at that handsome, beat-up face.

"What's the plan? Other than breakfast?" I asked as he

196

came up behind me and started massaging my shoulders. "God, that feels good."

"The plan is..." he said, dropping kisses along my neck, "we order room service—"

"I already like this plan," I interrupted.

"And then..." He stopped with the massage, turning me around to face him. "Look, I know you came here to get some space. Probably from me. But the thing is, we need space together, too. Away from all the bullshit back home."

Nodding, I said, "I know. It's a lot to deal with."

"So let's get away. From my parents and Claudia and even your family. You have your passport, right?"

"Yeah, but...exactly how far are we going?" I asked. "Will we be crossing time zones?"

Ford cupped my face in his hands and pressed a soft kiss to my lips. "It's a surprise. Do you trust me?"

"I—yes," I said.

He grinned. "Good. Why don't you hop in the shower while I order up some breakfast from room service, and then we'll eat and head out? I'll see if they have an avocado eggs benedict for you."

The man had memorized my go-to breakfast order. How could he not be a keeper?

"Sounds perfect," I told him.

By the time we got down to the lobby, I was bursting with excitement. And as it turned out, I had every reason to be.

After a short flight of less than one hour, Ford rented a car and drove us across the U.S. border to the Canadian side of Niagara Falls. I'd never been before, and the place was more majestic than I could have imagined.

"What do you think?" Ford asked as we pulled into the parking area. "Worth it?"

"God, yes. This is incredible," I said, already hanging halfway out the window to get a better view of the rainbows shimmering in the mist at the base of the falls.

After we parked, Ford took my hand and walked me right up to the rail beside the falls so we could hear the rush of the water pounding like thunder, feel the fine, cool spray hitting our faces. With all the natural beauty of the flora and fauna around us, I almost felt like I'd been transported to a magical land.

Ford got us ice cream cones, and we strolled around for a bit, window shopping and just enjoying each other's company. I was grateful he had suggested I bring my camera, because Niagara Falls was a photographer's dream. Not only was the landscape stunning to behold, but with all the tourists coming to see the falls, there were plenty of opportunities to take candid shots of excited pets and laughing kids. I couldn't wait to go over them later in our hotel room.

Pretty soon, my stomach was starting to rumble in earnest. It was getting close to dinner time, and the snacks we'd had on the plane hardly counted as lunch, in my book.

"Should we eat soon?" I asked.

"Don't you worry," Ford said, wrapping his arm around me. "Everything's under control. Speaking of which, we'd better head back to the car."

As if our trip to Niagara Falls wasn't romantic enough, Ford told me he'd made us a reservation for dinner at sunset at the Skylon tower, which had a slowly rotating dining room offering 360-degree views, perched almost a thousand feet off the ground. Sitting at our table, it really felt like we were floating directly above the falls. Thrilling and terrifying and wonderful all at once. Ford seemed amused by my inability to tear my gaze from the wall of windows and the spectacular bird's-eye view.

"Should I order for us?" he teased, refilling my wine-glass. "I think this is the first time I've ever seen you straight up ignore a restaurant menu."

"Ha ha," I shot back. "But seriously, this is just gorgeous. Thank you, Ford."

"Don't thank me. I didn't make the falls," he said with a smile.

"I mean it," I said, turning to look at him. "Thank you for this whole day."

Before I could say more, our waitress reappeared and—just as promised—Ford ordered for both of us. And he ordered half the menu, it seemed. Seared scallops over spinach, lobster tails with lemon garlic butter, steak, vegetable sides, crème brûlée and amaretto torte for dessert.

"You're a monster," I told him afterward. "There's no way we're going to be able to eat all of that."

"You should at least taste it all," he said. "I want you to have everything good."

"Do you?" I asked, raising a brow.

"I do."

He took my hands across the table, and I searched his eyes, seeing the sincerity there. His words seemed like they carried more weight than a casual dinner conversation would imply. Then the waitress came back to drop off a basket of hot bread and a plate of olive oil and herbs.

"Bet you're glad you brought your camera," Ford said as we tore the bread apart.

Nodding, I passed it over to him so he could click through some of the digital photos.

Laughing, he tilted the tiny screen toward me. "This one's great."

It was. A small Vietnamese boy, not more than four years old I'd guess, was chasing a flapping pigeon that had a French fry hanging from its mouth. I'd gotten that shot purely by luck.

But more than the camera, I realized, I was glad that I had Ford with me.

What was happening between us? It felt like more than friendship. More than sex. I wondered if I could trust it, trust him—if I could believe in us. One day didn't erase all the problems we'd had, the years of his manipulations and our unbalanced power dynamic. And who could say that Claudia wouldn't be back with her finger crooked at him?

Could I picture Ford truly standing up to his parents and declaring his love for me? Fighting to keep me, to keep our marriage intact? Honestly, no. I couldn't.

At the same time, I couldn't have pictured the sex we'd had last night either. The hand holding, the eye contact. Yet it had happened. *Today* had happened. Ford's hands had been on me ever since we woke up this morning, and his affection and warmth had continued all the way up until now. Our relationship had been such a roller-coaster ride, but one thing that seemed consistent was the way it was constantly shifting, deepening, strengthening. Through thick and thin, for better or worse, we were growing closer by the day. It was undeniable.

Still, I couldn't just abandon reality and jump whole-heartedly into the fantasy version of our marriage. The fact was, I had an agreement with the Malones to divorce Ford in less than a year. And that was after Ford had drawn up a contract with me that essentially said the same thing, though for very different reasons. This...thing between us, whatever it was, and no matter how nice it felt in the moment, was too good to be true in the long run. It wasn't meant to last.

But for today, I could pretend. Let myself forget the act, have one perfect vacation day, a second honeymoon—one where I could believe we were embarking on a fresh new beginning, rather than stealing a few quiet moments that would eventually have to end.

I was so entranced by the view of the sunset (and my tangled web of thoughts) that I couldn't make myself turn away from the candy-like splashes of color until I smelled the food being set down on our tablecloth.

"Everything looks so delicious," I practically moaned, my mouth watering.

"Make sure you save room for dessert," Ford reminded me with a wink.

The table was practically overflowing with French onion soup, perfectly cooked steak and lobster tails, fresh smoked Canadian salmon, the scallops, roasted zucchini and shiitakes. I didn't even remember Ford ordering half the dishes spread out before us.

As we ate, the sun dropped into the horizon, leaving trails of bright pink and orange across the sky. By the time our desserts came out, I wasn't even sure I'd be able to eat them.

"I don't know if I can stand another bite," I said, sighing as I looked down at the plates.

"Oh, I think you can," Ford said, picking up a spoon.

I watched as he tapped the crème brûlée, cracking the caramelized layer of burnt sugar on top, and then scooped up a perfect mouthful of custard and topping.

"Open wide," he said.

Blushing, I obeyed, and he slipped the spoon between

my lips, locking eyes with me as I sucked the dessert into my mouth.

"Mmm," I moaned. Glancing around the dining room, I realized we were at one of the only tables that was still occupied. It was almost like we had the restaurant all to ourselves. "Now the chocolate."

"As my lady commands," Ford said, smiling devilishly.

My husband went on feeding me dessert, kissing me between bites, and I reveled in the romance of it all as we sat perched among the stars, with eyes for nothing and no one but each other.

FORD

CHAPTER 26

We returned to Chicago, and time flew by in a glorious frenzy of sex and cozy companionship as Emzee and I reclaimed the strange little life we had been building. Our arrangement might have been unorthodox, but it worked for us. And for Munchkin.

Our morning breakfasts together had made a comeback, but with more talking and less reading our emails or mindlessly scrolling through our social media accounts. In fact, the apartment had almost become a screen-free zone, unless we were both working at our computers or watching a movie. When we were home, we were together.

Ever since the New York trip, I'd tried my best to be present and pay closer attention to my wife's wants and needs. When she mentioned that Munch was getting stinky, I took him to the groomer on my lunch break and surprised Emzee by bringing him home at the end of the work day with a fresh scent and a bandana around his neck. If she texted me about her bubble tea craving, I'd have one delivered to her office within the hour. Work stress got her down? I made time to draw her a bath or give her a massage.

Because whatever I had with her, I wanted to keep on having it. Which meant treating her like she mattered just as much as I did. It honestly wasn't much of a hardship, and it made me regret not giving her more consideration in the past. The truth was, I'd basically had my head up my ass for seven years. The girl of my dreams had been standing in front of me all along—I'd just been too self-absorbed to realize it. Now that I had her, I wasn't letting her go.

I also earned more brownie points when I taught a second workshop to a handful of the women from See Yourself who had expressed an interest in learning more about real estate. That wasn't the end of my good deeds, though. A few weeks later, after discussing the matter with Malone Real Estate Holdings' HR department, I was able to offer paid internships to two of the mentees who seemed to be the most promising prospects. Taking Emzee's advice into account, I even made sure the interns would be answering to a woman supervisor at MREH, to avoid any discomfort or potentially traumatic power dynamics. So far, things were working out great.

As for Emzee, she'd remained guarded in some respects, but beyond that she'd done everything I had asked and more. Hell, it was the *more* that was giving me so much hope.

She'd switched us back to real bacon after noticing that I was secretly feeding my portion of the turkey kind to Munchkin. She'd been practically taking notes in the bedroom, too. After one particularly hot blowjob, she'd made sure to repeat the move that got me off so hard—using her thumb to stroke the soft skin at the base of my balls while she was sucking—every time she'd given me head since. And when I had to work late, Emzee would hold off on watching our shows until I got home, so we could still watch them together over dinner.

Yet despite the fact that everything was going well, it all felt fragile.

If either of us were to actually acknowledge what was happening between us, try to talk about it or question it in any way, it might shatter everything. The relationship we were building wasn't a house of cards—it was a house of glass. Beautiful, delicate...and not necessarily built to last. No matter how much either of us might wish otherwise. But now, See Yourself's fundraiser was upon us, and I couldn't focus on anything else.

It was all Emzee had been able to think (and stress) about for the last week and a half, so even if I wanted to avoid worrying about the whole thing, it would have been impossible.

As we pulled up in front of my parents' meticulously kept brownstone mansion, I gave Em's hand a reassuring squeeze. There were still a few last-minute logistics to deal with.

"I'm so nervous I feel like I'm going to be sick," she said, huffing out a sigh.

"It'll be okay," I told her, putting the car in park and turning off the engine. "I'm sorry it's so uncomfortable for you. Just try to think about all the good it'll do for the nonprofit."

She nodded. "I know. It's gonna be worth it in the end. I mean, that's what's gotten me this far, right? It's just...ugh."

"Hard to accept help from snooty rich people?" I suggested.

"Especially snooty rich people who obviously don't like you. This is going to be the longest night ever." Her anxiety was so bad, I could see her hands shaking in her lap.

"My parents do like you," I soothed. "They're just...slow to warm up. Unlike me."

Then I pulled her in for a kiss, letting myself get lost in her soft lips and quiet moans for longer than I should have. Wishing more than anything that I could kiss her nerves away.

"Better get rid of that semi, Mr. Malone," Emzee whispered, dragging her hand over the bulge in my pants. "Though I wouldn't mind revisiting it later."

"Or we could just take care of it now..." I grinned suggestively. "We have time."

"As much as I'd love to have a quickie in the back seat of your car right outside your parents' house, I'm going to need every spare minute to get ready for this event," Emzee said.

"Then I'll take you up on that raincheck when we get home tonight."

I composed myself as quickly as possible and we headed up the front steps, holding hands as I rang the doorbell. The sound of it echoed from inside the house, and I could hear footsteps rushing down the stairs toward us.

"Here goes nothing," Emzee said under her breath, seconds before the door opened.

"Ford!" my parents' housekeeper Vivi exclaimed, reaching up to pat my cheek. "And sweet Mara. Lovely to see you both. Come in, dear hearts. I'll let them know you've arrived. Mara, do you want me to set your dress bag in an upstairs bedroom so you can get ready? Claudia's changing down the hall to the left, so I'll just put you in a room to the right."

"Thank you, that's perfect," Emzee said gratefully. "I'll be up shortly."

The housekeeper bustled away, and I leaned down to tell Emzee, "Vivi loves you."

"Vivi loves everybody," Emzee replied.

"Fair point," I conceded.

Vivi had always been the brightest, warmest thing in my parents' mansion. Growing up, the place had felt more like a museum full of rare antiques and expensive furniture and paintings than an actual house for a living, breathing family. Vivi's peanut butter cookies and kind counsel had made a difference, but even her goodness hadn't made up for the way my parents had always made me feel like an inconvenience—or a disappointment—to them.

Just then, Emzee's cell rang. She glanced down at the screen. "Shit. Don't be bad news."

"Who is it?" I asked.

"The caterer," she said, picking up. "Hello? ...This is she."

Emzee paced the hall, and from her end of the conversation I gathered that the caterer's fishmonger had raised the price on salmon but lowered the price of caviar. They were asking if she wanted to tweak the fundraiser's menu to avoid a several-thousand-dollar upcharge.

"I understand that," she was saying, visibly losing her cool, "but salmon with orzo is an entrée. Caviar with orzo is not. Do you see the problem?"

"Em—" I said, holding out a hand to take the phone.

Shaking her head, she looked down at her screen and her eyes got wide. "Let me call you right back," she said, tapping her screen and then holding it to her ear again. "Hello?"

It was the events manager at the Four Seasons. Their sound system was on the fritz and they weren't sure it would be repaired in time for the fundraiser in a few hours.

Were speeches with microphones necessary, or could Emzee get by with offering heartfelt greetings in the venue's foyer? The hotel was happy to print up any speeches or other informational materials to be set out on the tables, if it would help.

By the time my wife got off her second call from hell, sweat was beading at her temples and I could see her chest rising and falling with rapid breaths.

"Why don't you take a break?" I said, my hands on her shoulders. "I'll call the caterers first and then chew out the manager of the Four Seasons. A non-functional PA system is unacceptable, and if they can't provide one per your agreement, they'll have to make some calls and hire outside contractors to come in and set something up. But none of that is your job."

Nodding, Emzee said, "Maybe not my job, but it is my problem."

"Not for long. Just give me a few minutes to fix this," I told her. "I promise I'll make it better."

"But—"

"Nope," I said. "Now get that sexy ass upstairs and into that dress. I'll be up soon."

She sighed heavily, handing over her phone. "Thank you."

After she disappeared upstairs, I called the caterers to argue for a discount on the caviar option and have them swap it out with the scallop appetizer to make the scallops the main entree. This required the order of scallops to triple, but I worked in a discount for that as well.

Claudia was still upstairs, too busy primping (or pouting, more likely) to deal with any of these issues—which frankly should have been her purview, and I didn't need

Emzee to mention it for me to know it. Frankly, it was bad business.

And I didn't have to think too hard to guess why she had dropped the ball.

Ever since the night out for Roxana's birthday, I'd managed to avoid Claudia. It had been good for everyone—except Claudia, of course. She kept trying to worm her way back into my life, calling and texting me with questions about the fundraiser that should have been directed toward Emzee, but I just redirected them, refusing to respond to her in any capacity beyond my role as Emzee's husband who was helping her put the fundraiser together. I'd learned my lesson.

Playing into Claudia's hands in the past had done nothing but force my wife to flee into the arms of Andrew Apellido. The bruises on my face and the stitches above my eye had healed, but I wasn't going down that road a second time. I might have won the first round fight, but I wouldn't put myself in a position where I could lose Emzee again.

Unfortunately, the side effect of me avoiding Claudia was her using it as an excuse to avoid doing the work she had promised to do for See Yourself.

Mischief managed for the time being, I headed upstairs to check on Em. But she wasn't in the guest room that Vivi had set up for her, and her dress bag was still draped over the bed. The bathroom was unoccupied, so I surmised that she'd gone to speak with my parents. There was no way Emzee would be fraternizing with Claudia, after all.

Maybe it was a good thing. And if Emzee hadn't spoken to her about Claudia's behavior already, maybe I could get my mother to remind Claudia that she was supposed to be handling any and all last-minute SNAFUs for the fundraiser tonight. I'd genuinely thought that my ex would be a consummate professional, but apparently I had been wrong.

As for me, it was my job to make sure Emzee was aware of the time, get her zipped into her dress, and kiss her good luck. I'd hand her phone back over, but with the caveat that she would be fielding no more phone calls.

I started for my parents' bedroom at the far end of the hall, but as I approached the library, I slowed down, over-hearing stern voices coming from within.

The fucking library. I'd hated that room as a kid. Stuffed with impressive books that my parents had never actually read, it was the place where I'd always gotten lectures about how I wasn't living up to my "potential." Even in high school, that's where my parents would scold me about my future and every little thing I was doing wrong. More recently, they'd sat me down in there and tried to convince me to reconsider my breakup with Claudia.

"I have to say," I heard my mother saying coldly, "I'm extremely disappointed in your recent conduct."

Recent conduct? What was she talking about?

"You will recall, Mara, that we had a deal," my father said.

A deal? What possible deal could Emzee have with my parents? I moved closer.

"Now, we have already warned you that you'd better not get pregnant," my mother said. "But you two seem awfully close for a fake couple. So it seemed prudent to take this opportunity to remind you that this marriage ends cleanly."

My fists clenched, my stomach turning. I couldn't believe what I was hearing.

"If you get yourself pregnant, we'll have to say it isn't his," my father added.

My mother chimed in, "And trust us, darling, when we finish smearing you in the press, not even a DNA test will convince the world that our son is the father."

I stood there in the hallway, shock seeping into my system.

I'd never told my parents that it was a fake marriage.

Suddenly, the pieces started coming together, and I realized why Emzee had pulled away from me. Why things had changed between us so drastically after the wedding. Why her behavior had been so hot and cold, why she continued to put up walls and deny her feelings for me when, day by day, our connection felt so real.

It wasn't because of anything I'd done, or because she didn't truly care for me. It was because my parents had gotten involved. They had hated the idea of me marrying anyone but Claudia, so they'd pulled out all the stops and gone after Emzee to make sure we didn't stay together.

And the only way she would have gotten so tangled up in their web of deceit was if they had something on her. Something bad.

They'd been threatening her all along.

EMZEE

CHAPTER 27

Numb with shock, I was frozen to the floor as Mrs. Malone's words stabbed me in the gut. There was a cruel smirk on her face as she threatened me, saying that if I got pregnant, she'd tell the world I was a liar and that the baby wasn't Ford's.

Truthfully, starting a family wasn't something I had dared to think about much—not when I knew a divorce was looming in my future, not when my relationship with Ford was constantly giving me whiplash, and especially not when I hadn't grown up with the best parenting role model in my father. Plus, I still felt like a kid myself sometimes. I had no business trying to get pregnant. It certainly wasn't something I had been planning.

But the way the Malones were looking at me and speaking to me made me feel like a gold digger. Like trash. Did they actually think I was plotting to have Ford's baby?

If it weren't for the fundraiser tonight, I would have just run from the room and turned my back on the senior Malones for good. Nothing was worth the harassment I'd endured at their hands. I could spend the next nine or so months hunkered down at Ford's place, and simply make plans to be out of the house whenever they came over for their regular dinners with Ford.

I still couldn't tell my husband about the devil's bargain I'd made with his parents, or how they continued to blackmail me at every turn, but I could at least stay as far away from the Malones as possible. Set a firm boundary. After all, it was self-preservation. Even if Ford thought I was being unbearably rude, I'd stand my ground.

Then, without warning, he burst into the library.

"Oh, Ford dear," his mother said sweetly. "There you are. We were just—"

"Don't," he said, his voice cold.

I bit my lip, my eyes darting back and forth, my stomach in knots. I suspected by his tone, his expression, that he'd probably heard everything. That he understood what was going on—maybe not entirely, but enough to know that his parents had just been bullying me.

Ford moved to stand at my side, confirming my suspicions when he opened his mouth again to tell them off. "What have you done? What did you say to her?" he demanded.

"This is none of your concern," Mr. Malone said gruffly.

But my husband wasn't backing down. "It is, though. I heard enough from the hall. And I'd wager you two are the reason our relationship hasn't been able to move forward. So what do you have on her?"

My pulse quickened, adrenaline pumping hard. My secret was this close to being out.

"You don't know what you're talking about. You're being silly," Ford's mother said.

"I know how you two operate," Ford shot back, undeterred by her denials. "What are you threatening her with?"

"Threatening? How melodramatic. I'm sure we don't know what you're talking about," Mr. Malone scoffed. "Enough with these theatrics."

Ford's mother crossed the room with her hand out, but Ford flinched out of her reach. She shot me a glare.

"Tell him, Mara. Is there anything we could possibly be threatening you with?"

I was up against a wall and she knew it. There was obviously no way I was going to out myself to Ford. The last thing I wanted to do was admit that the Russian mob was after my whole family, and that the Malones' offer to pay them off—in exchange for agreeing to leave Ford—was the only way I could save us all.

"No," I said quietly, dropping my eyes to the floor.

"Em—" Ford said, turning me to face him. "Look at me."

"It's nothing," I insisted, but I couldn't meet his gaze and I knew he wasn't fooled.

Ford looked back at his parents. "You think I believe you?" he said. "I heard the words coming out of your mouths!"

He was livid. The anger I'd seen on his face when he found Andrew trying to make a move on me in the hotel hallway was nothing compared to this. Then, he'd been red faced and furious. Now, he was so angry that his entire body was radiating tension and danger, like a taut wire about to snap.

"Perhaps you misheard—" his mother began.

"No. I didn't," Ford said, interrupting. "So know this, both of you: Whatever you're trying to do, whatever you told Emzee, whatever you *think* is going to happen in the future—I am not giving her up. I will fight for the woman I love."

Love? Ford *loved me?* And this is how I was hearing it for the first time?

Mrs. Malone's mouth had fallen open, and I could see the shock in her eyes. I wasn't sure if Ford had ever spoken to her that way before.

I couldn't believe what I was hearing, either. Ford Malone had just said he loved me. Declared it forcefully. Was it real, or just for show? It felt real, but I was afraid to trust it.

"Son. There's no need for all this yelling. Let us explain," Ford's father tried, but Ford was having none of it —if anything, it seemed to stoke his anger even more.

"Fuck your explanations. Nothing you can say is going to drive us apart," Ford said.

If it *was* just a show, it was clear judging by the shock on his parents' faces that it had worked. That his words had done what they intended to do—get the Malones to back off. Because they didn't say another word as Ford took my hand and led me out of the room. His parents didn't try to stop us, didn't even try to argue.

As he whisked me down the hallway, back toward the guest room where I'd been getting ready, he lifted my hand to his lips and gently kissed the back of my knuckles. I was buzzing.

"I meant it, Emzee. Every word. I'm not going to let them come between us." We got to the room and he locked the door behind us, took a breath, and then looked down at me. "Please tell me you feel the same."

As if it was that easy.

I searched his eyes, and I knew he was being honest with me. But it wasn't as simple as us loving each other. The situation was much more complicated. My family was at risk without the Malones' support. The Bratva could hurt us. Financially, reputationally, even physically.

Right now, though, I was too moved—too in love—to deny what I was feeling.

"Ever since you rescued me seven years ago, I've been in love with you," I confessed.

Cupping my face, he drew me in for a kiss, so long and hard it took my breath away.

"I know," he said. "Or I thought I knew. I guess I didn't want things to change between us, and now...there's just so much I wish I would have done differently. God, I was an idiot."

I had to grin. "I would agree with that."

He sank onto the bed, taking me with him. His hands held mine tightly as if he was afraid to let me go. "Why didn't you tell me what was going on with them?"

Shaking my head, I said, "I didn't want to drive a wedge between you and your parents. I thought I could handle it. And I didn't think it mattered one way or the other."

It was the truth, even if it wasn't the whole truth. But I could tell Ford all about the Bratva later. We'd have plenty of time for the hard conversations now that he had committed himself to me. To us.

"It matters," Ford said, and then he was kissing me again like he never wanted to stop. My lips, my cheeks, my forehead, my throat. "I love you, Emzee."

"I love you too," I said.

He pulled me into his arms and we fell back onto the bed together, kissing and holding each other. We would probably be late for the fundraiser, but I didn't care.

As our kiss deepened, Ford helped me wiggle out of my clothes. When I was finally naked and stretched out on the bed, he stepped back to strip down and I watched him appreciatively, enjoying every inch of his gorgeous body. I didn't think I would ever get over the joy of knowing that he was mine. That he wanted me just as much as I wanted him.

By the time he was on top of me again, I was dripping wet. He let out a groan when he realized how ready I was for him.

"You feel so good on my hand," he whispered, fingering me as I grabbed his cock.

"I'm going to feel even better when you're inside me," I told him, nudging his hand aside and tugging his hard length down between my open legs.

He plunged inside easily, with one smooth, gliding motion, and I gasped as he stretched me wide, dipping his head down to take my nipple into his mouth. Using his tongue and his teeth, he teased me as his dick began pumping deeper and deeper. I was on fire for him. Every thrust felt deliciously perfect, the friction sending hot bolts of pleasure through both of us.

We were fucking desperately, hungrily, grinding hard against each other as we found our rhythm. I wanted him to fill me up completely.

"More," I murmured. "I want more."

He groaned as I wrapped my legs tight around his waist, pulling him even deeper inside.

"I can't—I'm going to come too fast," Ford warned.

"I want you to," I told him.

Our eyes met, and he increased the pace, his breath coming in short, harsh gasps.

"Come with me," Ford said.

"Yes."

I started moaning softly, and Ford covered my mouth with his. He pulled back to look me in the eyes again, and our connection was so hot and so intense that I felt tears welling up. I was overwhelmed by love and grateful we were together.

"I love you," I said.

"I love *you*," he said, kissing me again, his tongue matching the thrusts of his cock stroke for stroke. Faster and faster he pumped, and I slid my hands down to grip his firm ass, trying to drive him even deeper inside me.

"Yes, yes, yes," I moaned, closing my eyes and letting the sensations overwhelm me.

Suddenly the rippling wave of my orgasm started to spill over, and I could feel the moment it started happening, bursts of pleasure twisting inside me, unstoppable now, my pussy clenching around him.

"Ford," I panted, blinking back tears.

"Fuck yes, Emzee," he groaned, pumping faster and faster. "I'm coming."

He shuddered as he let go inside me, coming in short, breathless jerks, and I dug my fingers into his shoulders to hold him even tighter. It felt like there was nothing else in the world as we climaxed in each other's arms. Just me and Ford and the love we shared.

EMZEE

CHAPTER 28

"Better finish getting ready, love," Ford was saying, rubbing my back. "The fundraiser awaits. I think if we hurry, we might even get there on time."

Letting out a drowsy sigh I sat up, smiling at my husband. "Let's hop to it, then."

I was satiated and happy—so, so happy—but I still needed to make it through tonight's event. After that, no more bending over backwards to stay on the good side of Claudia and Ford's parents. I had no idea what the future held, but I promised myself that I was going to meet it bravely. Even if that meant rocking the boat a little.

Or a lot.

"Your dress?" Ford said, handing me the garment bag. He had already slipped into his tux, which took him all of three minutes flat. I envied him.

"Thank you," I said. "Can you hand me my purse? My MAC lipstick is in there."

"As the lady wishes."

But when I propped the bag open, I saw something

tucked in there that I'd somehow forgotten about. The Test. Because I was a tiny bit late.

I was sure I had nothing to worry about, but after the brouhaha with Ford's parents, I was on edge. I figured now was as good a time as any to just take it, confirm what I already knew, and be done with it. That way I could banish the niggling worry in the back of my mind.

Grabbing my lipstick, I palmed the test and slipped them both into my makeup bag. Then I zipped it up and tucked it under my arm.

"You know what?" I said, trying to sound casual. "I think I'll fix my hair and makeup in the bathroom, and then you can help me into my dress afterward. Shouldn't take too long."

"Sure," he said from the wingback chair he was sitting in, glancing up from his phone with a smile. "And try not to stress. You already look perfect."

He had no reason to be suspicious of me; the guest bath down the hall had a luxurious full vanity with a cushioned velvet bench and a bunch of those Hollywood-style round bulbs spaced out around the mirror. It was basically fit for a princess. I'd mooned over it as a teenager.

I kissed him on the cheek, adjusted his bow tie, and headed down the hall.

First things first, I locked myself in and peed on the stick. I was supposed to get my results in five minutes, so I set it on the back of the toilet tank and then busied myself doing my makeup in front of the vanity.

Luckily, I didn't need to do a full face, just freshen up my skin with some blotting paper and powder and spend a few minutes turning my daytime eyes and lips into evening look. Liquid eyeliner, a fresh coat of mascara, and a swipe of deep burgundy eyeshadow later, I was just about ready to check on the test when I heard a knock.

"Just a sec," I called out, assuming it was Ford coming to check on me.

But when I opened the door, it was Claudia, her blonde hair gleaming, her midnight blue evening gown flowing around her in a rustling cloud of tulle.

My stomach dropped. "Um. Can I help you?"

"I need to use this bathroom," she said.

"There's another one right down the hall," I told her, still standing in the door. I fought the urge to add, "So you can fuck directly off." There were probably half a dozen bathrooms in the Malones' mansion—she had to know that. Yet she'd busted into this one.

Claudia let out a huge sigh, rolling her eyes. "I need to use *this* bathroom," she repeated. "It has the good mirror. The best one in the whole house, you know." She paused to give me a smug, self-satisfied look. "Actually, I guess you *wouldn't* know. You haven't really spent that much time here, have you?"

Of course she had to remind me how well acquainted she was with the house and all the people in it. But the joke was on her. I'd known Ford years longer than Claudia had, and I sure as hell knew this was the money mirror. The last thing I wanted to do was start a fight about it, though. Especially not with the fundraiser less than an hour away.

Shoving her way past me in a most unladylike fashion, Claudia flounced over to the vanity and leaned over to study her reflection. My eyes darted to the toilet in the corner. I silently prayed she wouldn't suddenly decide she had to use it, because if she turned around, there was no way she'd miss the pink plastic pregnancy test sitting right there.

Unsurprisingly, however, she was completely focused on her makeup and oblivious to me and my nerves. Thank God.

"You look great," I told her, partly to keep the peace but mostly to try coaxing her the hell out of there.

"I know," she said breezily, ignoring my attempts to get her out the door. "Is that MAC?"

Her evil gaze had lit upon my prized red lipstick.

"It's Viva Glam," I said.

She was taking up too much space, dabbing on my lipstick and then frowning at it like it was distasteful, talking nonstop the whole time.

"Ew. This is way too plum for me. I guess it's meant for people with really pasty skin, like you. Pass me a cotton ball so I can get it off."

I sat back down on the bench and handed her a few cotton balls, hoping to get her on her way, but she continued fussing with her hair and lips as if we had all the time in the world. I'd never felt so claustrophobic. Her body, her heavy white floral perfume, and her voluminous dress were physically blocking me in against the wall. I couldn't have gotten away if I'd tried.

"It's so weird you and Ford ended up together, isn't it?" she asked, releasing a violent cloud of hairspray in my direction.

Waving it away, I said, "What do you mean?"

If anything, I'd always thought of our relationship—real or not—as the kind of thing that people assumed was just inevitable. We'd been close friends for almost a decade.

Claudia shrugged. "Oh, well, you know. With everything that happened to you back in high school."

"You didn't even go there," I pointed out. "And what's so weird about longtime friends getting together?"

She turned to look at me pityingly. "I'm his longtime friend too, Em."

A flash of anger rippled through me hearing my nickname. I didn't like anyone calling me Em that wasn't a good friend or a family member. Claudia was neither. Not by a long shot.

"I remember him telling me all about the way you latched onto him back in tenth grade. His little sucker fish, right? Cute."

My face went hot. "Well, I wouldn't...I mean, that's not—"

"I just find it really ironic, considering," she went on.

Fine. I would bite. "Considering what?"

She turned to face me, staring down from her willowy height, made even more impressive by her stilettos. Judging by the smile on her face, it was clear I had just walked right into a trap.

"Oh, you know." She looked at her nails, pretending to be casual. "Considering that he'd written all those nasty slurs about you in the locker room after he found out that *your* father had been supplying *his* with whores."

A shockwave went through me. "What?"

"Oops!" Claudia said. "I mean 'sex workers.' We don't want to be bad feminists, do we? Well. See you out there!"

With that, she gave me a condescending pat on the shoulder and then sauntered out, leaving me stunned and sick to my stomach.

I was staggered, caught between devastation and disbelief. Could it possibly be true?

Ford was the one who had started the bullying all those years ago?

Ford had known about my father's human trafficking

ring before I did—before anyone in my family did—and he had done nothing?

The floor was dropping out from under me. I ran back to the toilet and sank to my knees in front of it, lightheaded and still nauseated. I didn't throw up, but it took me a few minutes to calm down as I realized that my entire relationship with Ford, *from day one*, had been based on a bigger lie than I could have ever imagined.

And as much as I wanted to believe Claudia had made it all up, the only way she could have known any of those things was if Ford had told her.

I got to my feet shakily and took a deep breath. Just as I was convinced that things couldn't possibly get any worse, my eyes settled on the thing I had completely forgotten about. The only thing that could be more important than what I'd just heard.

The plus sign on my now-positive pregnancy test.

Don't miss the conclusion of Emzee and Ford's story...

My family has given everything to salvage the Zoric name and reputation from my father's tarnished legacy.

I only needed a moment to destroy it all.

Along with two hearts.

It was supposed to be a simple charade. I never thought Ford and I would fall in love.

But I can't take back what I've done.

He can't change the past.

And what we've done changes everything.

But only if I stop running.

Someone has to lose either way. But when the truth comes out, it might just be all of us.

Find out what happens in The Truth.

PAIGE PRESS

Paige Press isn't just Laurelin Paige anymore...

Laurelin Paige has expanded her publishing company to bring readers even more hot romances.

Sign up for our newsletter to get the latest news about our releases and receive a free book from one of our amazing authors:

Stella Gray
CD Reiss
Jenna Scott
Raven Jayne
JD Hawkins
Poppy Dunne

ABOUT THE AUTHOR

Stella Gray is an emerging author of contemporary romance. When she is not writing, Stella loves to read, hike, knit and cuddle with her greyhound.

f ⊙